Julie Bozza

The Valley
of the Shadow
# of Death

LIBRAtiger

Revised edition published by LIBRAtiger 2017

ISBN: 978-1-925869-23-1

First published by Homosapien Books 2001, and by Manifold Press 2011

Text: © Julie Bozza 2017
Proof-reading and line editing: Two Marshmallows | twomarshmallows.net
Editor: Fiona Pickles, Manifold Press
Print format: © Julie Bozza 2017
Set in Adobe Caslon

Cover image: © Sawyer Bengtson | unsplash.com
Cover design: © Julie Bozza 2017

libra-tiger.com | juliebozza.com

DEDICATION

for DM
with infinite gratitude

CHAPTER ONE

Delaney's new partner was impatient with him. But Delaney didn't take the situation personally, for it seemed that Officer Robert Watson was impatient with everything in his world and had been for a very long time, and had no intention of quitting any day soon.

The West Side of Chicago wasn't an easy place in which to be a police officer, after all. Joshua Delaney had discovered as much within hours of moving there, so he could understand that years of working in the thirty-third precinct had diminished Watson's tolerance levels. Especially when burdened with a country hick for a new partner.

It could not be said that their styles meshed. Delaney and Watson had, however, found ways of working together without the latter murdering the former, despite Watson often muttering, "What's one more dead cop washed up on the shores of Lake Michigan? No one would notice." Delaney figured that when all was said and done, they were both, in their own ways, good police officers. What more did they really need?

When the pair's eight-hour shift ended at midnight, they were in the habit of walking out of the police station together, both still wearing their blue uniforms, displaying more solidarity than actually existed. Somehow, Watson always managed to find a parking space on the street just outside the station house and Delaney would accompany his partner to the man's car before walking back to his apartment alone.

Tonight, Watson was opining on the necessity of experience. "You're just too green, Delaney. If you ever survive to my age, if you see a bit of life, *then* you might cope with Chicago."

Delaney kept his tone mild and even. "I'm thirty-two, Robert. I'm only ten years behind you."

Watson threw an irritated grimace in his direction. "Thirteen years," Watson corrected him. "And you act like you're a rookie."

"I haven't been a rookie since I turned twenty. It's not as if I don't have experience."

"Yeah, but only out in the sticks."

"That counts," Delaney asserted. Then he shrugged. "Though I can't deny everything's different here. I've never worked in a city even half this size, I've never had a long term partner."

"Fuck … it's not even like you were in a different time zone; you came here from a different *era*! This is the nineties, you know. The *nineteen nineties*."

"I am aware of it," Delaney mildly replied.

As Watson unlocked his car he summarized his point of view. "You'll learn, Delaney. But you'll have to learn quick, this is the deep end they threw you into."

Delaney nodded a farewell, and began to walk off.

That wasn't the end of Watson's good advice, however. While pulling away from the curb, the man powered down the window and called out, "And for God's sake, get yourself a new car!"

"Maybe," Delaney replied, lifting his hand in acknowledgement. It hadn't been an auspicious beginning for the police officer new to Chicago, having his car stolen almost right out from under his nose. He had no idea when he'd be able to afford a replacement – and, strangely enough, he felt little inclination to buy one anyway.

"Damned fool," Watson muttered as he drove off, apparently not caring that Delaney could hear him. Then Delaney's partner was gone. The forever-busy police station was already behind him – Delaney turned the next corner and was alone.

The West Side of Chicago seemed to be constructed from contradictions. In many ways, it was a family neighborhood; full of houses and churches and schools and shops. Lights were on in the homes that Delaney walked past, but the doors and windows were dauntingly secured, so the overall effect wasn't welcoming. The restaurants and clubs scattered throughout the area were busy, and cars sped or crawled along the streets, but there weren't many people out on the sidewalks. Apparently it was considered wise to opt for the relative safety of being inside a vehicle or a building. Delaney strode on, passing a row of shops all closed and barricaded for the night, and then a few dark warehouses.

The next two blocks were given over to a cramped and jumbled industrial area. Beyond that were a couple of cheap office buildings, then more houses, and finally Delaney's apartment block. It seemed he would be delayed, however, despite his shabby home and uncomfortable bed beckoning – for a good police officer was never off duty, and there were laws being broken here.

Delaney stood for a moment and contemplated the situation. A number of cars were parked haphazardly outside one of the warehouses, spilling into the street with no regard for anyone else's convenience. The whole thing was typical of the Chicago 'fuck you' attitude.

First, Delaney wrote tickets for the car that was blocking a fire hydrant and for the others parked on the sidewalk. And then he became engrossed in jotting down the registration numbers of the remaining cars. There seemed to be no one else around and he hadn't been expecting trouble, so Delaney was startled when he heard someone comment, "Christ, this is all we need." He looked around to discover three men standing a few yards away, two of them holding Delaney at gunpoint.

"Tonight of all nights," another one added with much the same impatient inflections as Watson used. "First Trezini and now a cop."

The first man indicated the warehouse with a tilt of his chin. "Get in there," he said.

There seemed little Delaney could do but obey. With slow deliberate movements, he slid his pen into one pocket and his notepad into another. And then, holding both hands palm-out in plain view, he led the way towards the only doorway he could see.

Angelo Trezini was slowing down, too cold and too dull to even think. Well, his only thought was a wistful wish for the energy necessary to feel sad or sorry or righteously pissed off. He was fading fast.

He was in a freezer. A large storage room of a freezer, packed high with cartons of food, and lit so brightly that Trezini was forced to squint. When his eyes were open, that is. Mostly he was just pacing in a circle, eyes shut tight against the harsh light and harsher cold, arms wrapped around his chest. He'd lost count of the number of times he'd walked this circle, but it was often enough that he didn't have to look where he was going anymore.

A muffled clang, and the door swung open. It all happened so fast, and Trezini was feeling so slow that he didn't have a chance to take advantage of the situation. As luck would have it, he was as far away as his circle took him – by the time he'd turned and drawn his gun, the door was already slamming shut again. And Trezini had company.

He was staring down his gun-barrel at a big dumb hunk of a man wearing a cop's uniform. A man who was so ridiculously handsome that Trezini almost forgot the cold for a moment. There was a stillness about the man, a sense that he was completely self-contained.

The two men considered each other for a time; neither making any untoward moves, though Trezini aiming a gun at him didn't seem to faze the cop. Wisely, even though the cop held a gun loosely in his own hand, he made no attempt to lift it; he hadn't even instinctively tightened his grip. After a still moment, the cop carefully turned the butt of the handle towards Trezini to show him that the clip was missing, presumably confiscated. Maybe the morons who'd put Trezini in here had already learned one lesson.

Eventually, as the cop lowered his hand to hang harmlessly by his side, Trezini demanded, "Who the hell are you?"

"Officer Joshua Delaney, thirty-third precinct."

"Yeah, the pleasure's all mine," Trezini sarcastically responded. "What are you doing here?"

Speaking in an unexpectedly conversational tone, the man explained, "Well, I assume someone didn't appreciate me issuing parking tickets. There were cars parked illegally outside the warehouse."

Parking tickets? Trezini didn't bother hiding his disbelief. "What, are you feeling suicidal? This isn't the part of town to get nosy in."

"I'm new to Chicago." There was still a complete lack of self-consciousness, despite being so badly caught out.

The guy was patently harmless, so Trezini re-holstered his gun, noting that his companion's self-possession remained constant despite the withdrawal of this threat. "Yeah, that would explain why you're in this neighborhood at this time of night, trying to ticket wiseguys for letting their meters run out."

"Blocking a fire hydrant," the cop corrected him, "parking too close to an intersection, and parking on the sidewalk." He let a beat go by before asking, "These people are mobsters?"

Trezini let out a laugh. "Don't get too excited – this bunch are nothing more than associates and wannabes. Total amateurs." As requested, the cop remained unexcited, though the frown tilted towards Trezini indicated that he was certainly curious. Trezini asked him, "You'd still have given them tickets, wouldn't you, even if you knew? You'd still be nosy."

Delaney shrugged, as if this was of no importance. "Yes." His breath fogged whenever he spoke.

Belatedly realizing he'd started shivering again, Trezini recommenced pacing around his circle, hugging himself ineffectually. He closed his eyes against this harsh fate.

The cop commented, "We're in danger of dying from hypothermia."

Trying to generate the heat of sarcasm, Trezini said, "Quick, aren't you? They'd have taken my gun if they planned on me surviving." He shrugged, though his shoulders were already stiff. "Or maybe they panicked, they just didn't think, and now they have to let the freezer do their work for them."

"Then we have at least two advantages."

"What?"

A hint of humor kicked up one corner of the cop's mouth. "They didn't search me. I have a spare clip."

"Being armed ain't gonna count for much when we're dead."

"Here." When Trezini opened his eyes again, he found that the cop was shrugging off his woolen coat while looking about him at the freezer's interior. "Take this," the guy said, absently holding the coat out towards Trezini.

Well, Trezini was hardly going to refuse it, though he was suspicious of such noble generosity.

Noticing this momentary hesitation, the cop explained, "You're far slimmer than I am, and you're only wearing a suit; you need it more."

"Sure. Who's arguing?" Trezini grabbed the coat, put it on over his suit jacket and buttoned it up. Unfortunately the extra layer didn't seem to make much difference: perhaps Trezini was already too cold, and couldn't warm up again.

Delaney seemed oblivious to the discomfort, though his warmest garment now was a knitted woolen sweater. While the two men were both about six feet tall, the cop certainly had the larger frame, giving the rather attractive impression of solid muscle and perhaps a little excess padding. Turning the collar up and huddling gratefully into the coat, Trezini dismissed the cop for his stupidity while also reluctantly admiring him for his decency.

The cop checked that the door was indeed locked, the safety handle disabled. And then he began looking around the freezer; as he went, he absently reloaded his gun, and chambered a bullet. Trezini watched him with little interest, having already searched for escape routes. Well, Trezini watched him with the interest anyone reserved for men who were movie-star handsome, though it was really far too cold for any reaction beyond a vague appreciation.

There were no exits other than the locked door, but there was a grated vent high on one wall. The cop hauled a few cartons of frozen food over and stacked them so that he could climb up to the vent. Guessing what the guy was intending, Trezini wrestled some of the modular metal shelving apart and handed Delaney a sturdy bar.

The grate was soon prized off, and the cop was leaning inside. But, "It's no use," the guy announced. "This duct leads straight up for twenty feet, we'd never climb it."

Well, Trezini hadn't really been hoping for much, anyway. The cop scrambled down again, and continued exploring – leaving the cartons, grate and bar where they were. Trezini watched him surreptitiously, beginning to get curious. Who the hell was this guy?

"We must have both surprised them," Delaney eventually said. He produced a folded-up blanket from a cabinet near the door. "They didn't remove the first aid kit and, luckily for us, it contains a blanket."

Trezini frowned at him, wondering what the cop would come up with next, and pondering the problem with this scenario. "Of course," he sighed. "There's only one blanket."

It was vital to remain conscious and to keep moving. Delaney considered the situation at length, trying to think of anything else they could do to help ensure their survival, but he figured they were already doing everything they could.

The two men had the blanket wrapped snugly around their shoulders, and were pacing around in a clear area near the door – pacing the same circle Trezini said he'd covered a hundred times already. "This is getting monotonous," the man grumbled. "We're going to wear a groove in the floor." They each had an arm round the other's waist, and it was apparent that Trezini was far less comfortable with this proximity than Delaney.

Delaney turned his thoughts to his companion. It seemed they were much the same age, though Trezini's hairline was already receding. He wasn't a handsome man, though he had a slim and attractive figure. His suit and shirt appeared to be expensive; their style and colors were subtle and flattering. As for Trezini's likely occupation … Breaking the silence, Delaney asked, "Are you a mobster, too?"

"What if I am?" was the immediate retort.

Their current situation demanded a rearrangement of the usual priorities. Delaney asked, "Is there any chance of you being rescued?"

Trezini shrugged within the confines of the blanket and Delaney's embrace. "No one but my Ma will miss me until morning. These guys are bringing all kinds of trouble down on their heads, but that'll be too little too late for me. What about you?"

"No one will miss me," Delaney said in the steadiest of tones, "and nobody knows I'm here."

Trezini cast him a disparaging glance. "So, you're going to die because of parking violations."

"And why are you here?"

"Well, I guess I don't have any better a reason – I was collecting protection money." Trezini went on to belligerently admit, "Yes, all right, I'm a wiseguy, I work for the establishment. But these morons are developing their own agenda, and I wandered in at the wrong time."

Despite himself, Delaney was a tad surprised. He'd initially assumed Trezini didn't play a significant role in this city, though perhaps Delaney was guilty of underestimating the man. "You work for Matthew Picano?"

Trezini shoved Delaney away, keeping the blanket around his own shoulders. "Oh yeah," he said with great sarcasm, "you're real new to Chicago." And the man strode on, muttering a pithy comment to himself.

Delaney stood there alone in the cold, watching his volatile companion. At last he asked, "Will you tell me your name?"

"Why not. What have I got to lose? Trezini. Carmine Angelo Trezini. And if you try to use what I said as evidence, I'll deny everything. You didn't Mirandize me, anyway."

"I'm really not interested in arresting you, Mr. Trezini," Delaney mildly replied.

"Of course not. We're going to die instead." Another turn round his circle as this thought sank in. Then Trezini glanced over at Delaney, and relented. "Oh, come here."

Delaney joined Trezini under the blanket where they fitted themselves close together again, and kept walking.

Trezini seemed less wary now that the truth was out – and he also seemed mildly amused, though Delaney wasn't sure whether the humor was generated by the situation, by Delaney, or by Trezini himself. They walked on, going nowhere, in companionable silence.

Time meant very little. It took a while for Delaney to notice that their pace was significantly slower, that he and Trezini were both hunched over now, and that they were very much relying on each other's support. Such obliviousness could be dangerous. With an effort, he said, "Talk to me, Mr. Trezini. Tell me something about yourself."

"No, you first," the man replied. "Tell me – what's a nice boy like you doing in nasty old Chicago?"

Delaney grimaced to himself. "I moved here after turning in a number of officers for drug-running, bribery and murder. The city doesn't hold a monopoly on corruption."

Trezini was staring hard and disbelieving at him, from a mere breath away. "You turned in your own people? In my line of business, you get transferred directly to hell for that, do not pass go, do not collect two hundred dollars."

"My line of business has hardly been forgiving. They wanted me to resign right away, but I wouldn't – at least, not until I'd won the position here."

"I wanted to be a cop."

Delaney looked at the man beside him, skeptical of this unexpected statement.

Trezini, however, was a bit wide-eyed, as if taken aback by his own plain-spoken honesty. After a moment, he plunged ahead with an explanation. "When I was a kid, it was all I ever wanted to be." He let out a laugh as he said, "We'd play cops and robbers, and I'd be the only guy on the right side of the law. But Matthew's father ran the neighborhood, and my Dad was his right-hand man. So, when I was eighteen, Matt offered me work, and of course I said yes."

Frowning, Delaney asked, "But if you wanted to be a cop … ?"

Trezini shrugged. "It wouldn't have been the thing to do, people wouldn't have understood. And my Dad would have completely disowned me – not that we ever really got it together before he died. Anyway, Matt was the in-crowd, and I was tired of being outside. What else could I have done?"

"Well, Mr. Trezini, you could have become the man *you* wanted to be."

But apparently that was too blunt a challenge: the mobster's expression changed from candid to a guardedness betraying only annoyance. Cold silence returned, and the pair kept walking.

An uncounted number of circuits later, Delaney belatedly realized that he and Trezini were barely shuffling along. It was time to make a conscious decision or two while they still could. "Stop," Delaney muttered. "We need to stop."

"Need to keep moving," Trezini reminded him.

"No, we can't walk for much longer. We should stop now, while we know what we're doing."

"I don't know what I'm doing …"

They kept trudging slowly around. Eventually Delaney continued, "It's a risk, Mr. Trezini, but I think we should stop and bundle up together in the blanket. If we hold each other close, we can share our body heat."

"I don't think I've got any left to share," the man replied, and it was apparent that he was aware enough to be sarcastic, to try to control the stutter caused by chattering teeth. It was another ten steps before Trezini reluctantly agreed. "Well, all right. I suppose we have nothing to lose except our dignity."

Delaney had already chosen the best place: a corner tucked away near the door but out of sight of anyone coming through it; they would be on the opposite side of the room from the vent he'd opened. He now steered them both slowly towards it, breaking out of their circle.

Trezini was numbly cooperative. He said, "If we're going to die in each other's arms, we should at least be on a first-name basis. What do your friends call you?"

"Delaney. Or Joshua."

"Josh it is," the man decided. "As for me – well, no one calls me Carmine, that was my father's name."

Having reached his chosen corner, Delaney set Trezini to stand by himself for a moment.

The slimmer man waited patiently, huddled within the cop's too-large coat, rambling on about his name. "Ma calls me Angelo, because I'm her angel. Matthew calls me Cat, from my initials."

With cold-stiffened fingers, Delaney arranged the blanket around his shoulders, then leaned back against the wall, and opened his arms. Once Trezini had moved into his embrace, Delaney wrapped the blanket tightly around him so that they were cocooned together. He asked, "What do your friends call you, Mr. Trezini?"

"The people I work with call me Trez."

"What would you like me to call you?"

Trezini stared directly at him for a long moment, despite the nose-to-nose proximity. At last the man answered, "Angelo."

"Thank you," Delaney said. They were settled now, standing there holding each other so much closer than two men could possibly be comfortable with – but they were also as protected from the cold as they could manage for now. Although Trezini had his arms folded protectively across his own chest, his gaze was piercingly curious. Delaney offered, "If you lower your head to my shoulder, Angelo, I could cover it with this corner of the blanket."

"No," the man replied, his voice a shade rougher. "No, if I'm going to die, I may as well do it looking at you. God in His mercy must have sent you to ease my way."

Delaney returned his gaze with a frown, unsure what was intended by such a statement, and uncertain how to respond to it. He was further confused when Trezini tilted his head and leaned forward to press his mouth against Delaney's in a one-sided kiss. A disconcerting moment of intimacy stretched. Delaney had no idea how best to react.

At last, Trezini pulled back.

Delaney found his voice and said, "Why don't you talk to me? Or recite something, a speech or a song or a poem. The Declaration of Independence."

Taking this suggestion seriously, and apparently willing to be diverted, Trezini whispered, "All I know is prayers and confessions." His lips moved silently for a moment, and then he began reciting. "We have left undone those things which we ought to have done; And we have done those things which we ought not to have done; And there is no health in us."

"Could we try for something a little more cheerful?"

Trezini thought for a moment, and continued, "To you, O Lord, I lift up my soul. Let me not be ashamed; Let not my enemies triumph over me. Do not remember the sins of my youth, nor my transgressions; According to your mercy remember me."

"This is how you pray?" Delaney carefully asked.

"They're psalms."

Delaney took a breath and said, "Are you ashamed of who you are, Angelo? Because I believe that redemption is the stuff of life. You could still become the man you wanted to be."

Trezini was slowly shaking his head in denial. "No, it's too late for that."

"If you want to redeem your soul, Angelo, work with me."

"How am I supposed to do that?"

The answer seemed obvious to Delaney. "Give me the evidence I need to help the federal authorities deal with Matthew Picano as he deserves. We can work together to bring him down."

Trezini's smile was wry, though it lacked sharpness. It seemed that now he'd stopped moving, Trezini was really losing his focus to the cold. "And what do I get out of that?" he asked after a moment. "Other than a direct transfer to hell. Not that we're not dead already."

"Redemption."

The smile grew sweeter. "Don't get me wrong, a direct transfer to heaven would be an improvement. But all I want to do right now is sleep. Sleep with you." Trezini leaned a fraction closer, so that he rested against Delaney forehead-to-forehead. And he confessed in a whisper, "I feel warm now."

"I know it's tempting," Delaney bluntly announced, "but if you give in to that and fall asleep, you'll die."

Trezini's attention was successfully caught; he lifted his head and stared at his companion.

Delaney explained, "You feel warm when you freeze to death."

"But that's so unfair!" Trezini sounded outraged.

A long moment stretched, and Delaney made a confession of his own. "I fear it's actually rather pleasant, beyond a certain point."

"Pleasant?" Trezini echoed. He turned away for a moment – not that he could go far – and then met Delaney's gaze. "Do you know, Josh, I thought the warmth was me falling in love with you."

Taken aback by this statement, Delaney just stared at the man. The whole idea was so unexpected that he didn't even grasp the shape of it yet, hadn't even found a name for it. Trezini was shifting, stiffly untangling his arms and insinuating them around Delaney's waist. And then the weight of Trezini's body pressed against his, and that sensual mouth met Delaney's again.

Delaney refused to cooperate. When Trezini broke the kiss, Delaney said, "Please don't do that, Angelo. I'm not –"

"Then don't talk to me about redemption," the man retorted.

"But I want you to work with me against Picano."

Trezini groaned, and let his head fall to rest against Delaney's shoulder. "I'm dying, Josh, stop pestering me."

"You are not dying," Delaney said: "I won't let you."

But it seemed that Trezini had drifted away.

"Angelo … Angelo?"

No reply.

Delaney managed to free an arm, and carefully lifted Trezini's head. The man's eyes were closed in sleep or unconsciousness. Needing to regain Trezini's attention, and figuring that desperate times called for desperate measures, Delaney clumsily kissed him. "Angelo!"

Nothing.

Another kiss, and at last Trezini responded, his mouth on Delaney's vague yet hungry. "Stay with me," Delaney said, "talk to me."

Those lips moved, though the eyes remained hooded. After a moment, Trezini's words became recognizable. "The Lord is my shepherd; I shall not want."

Delaney joined in, though at first he was uncertain of the words, for it seemed his school had taught a more modern version of the psalm. Together he and Trezini recited, "He maketh me to lie down in green pastures; He leadeth me beside the still waters. He restoreth my soul …"

Time passed. The two men repeated the psalm again and again, though it became more and more of an effort as they fought off the cold. "… And I will dwell in the house of the Lord For ever …"

"The Lord is my shepherd; I shall not want …" Awful, how sluggish Trezini became – at times, his words slurred almost beyond recognition. Delaney tried to shift his arms every now and then without losing his grip on the blanket; providing friendly embraces of Trezini's shoulders, inexpert caresses of his waist, endeavoring to keep the man interested in remaining alive. "… He leadeth me in the paths of righteousness For His name's sake."

The door was opening.

Delaney quit reciting, not wanting to be overheard, blearily trying to listen for footsteps and thereby work out how many people he would have to deal with.

Oblivious, Trezini was mumbling on. "Yea, though I walk through –"

The quickest way to hush him was for Delaney to press his mouth to Trezini's. A still moment with their lips crushed together, and then Trezini's eyes opened. Delaney pulled away, and with a tilt of his head drew the man's attention to the fact that they had company.

Waking up a little further, Trezini blinked a time or two, slow to catch up. But finally he widened his eyes and nodded; a serious set to his jaw indicated that he was ready for a fight. They both knew there would be no second chances.

Delaney let the blanket drop away. He and Trezini each stood alone, regaining their balance, stiffly trying to roll and shrug movement back into their shoulders. Both of them drew their guns.

A glance around the corner they were hidden behind revealed that four hoods had entered the freezer; the three men who'd thrown Delaney in, and one more. Apparently they were expecting to find a pair of frozen corpses, for none of the four had drawn their weapons. Puzzled, the hoods spread out, searching for their captives. Two of them headed towards the cartons stacked under the open vent, though they soon realized that Delaney and Trezini couldn't have escaped that way.

Another of the hoods – Delaney recognized him as the first who'd spoken when they'd found him noting down registration numbers – was walking towards Delaney and Trezini's hiding place. As soon as the hood was within reach, Delaney swung out and hit him over the head with the weight of his gun. The man dropped, unconscious.

Trezini immediately followed this up by firing at the hood who was furthest away – and managed to hit him. The second man also dropped to the floor.

That evened the odds, with only two hoods remaining now, but Delaney and Trezini were relatively incapacitated and no longer possessed the element of surprise.

Trezini fired at the other hood over by the cartons, but with less success; perhaps Trezini had by now recalled that he was only half-alive. And the shots were returned, which led to a dilemma – the only cover available would lead them further into the room and away from the door, but it was imperative that Delaney and Trezini not get shut in the freezer again. It would literally be the death of them.

There was really only one option – Delaney decided that an all-or-nothing assault was called for. Trezini was still firing at the man furthest away – Delaney began firing as well, while running at the nearest hood and tackling him. All was confusion for endless moments …

The crazy cop wrestled his goon to the floor – and the goon Trezini had in his sights backed away as Delaney's inertia threatened to bowl him off his feet, too. Trezini took advantage of the brief lull in gunshots, grabbed for a carton of food and threw it at his man – who successfully ducked, which was hardly surprising. Trezini wasn't exactly quarterback material right now.

Trouble was, his goon was now heading towards the door. And Trezini did *not* want to get locked in here again. He took a step, but was pinned in place with another couple of shots. The goon was almost free.

Delaney and his goon were wrestling back and forth on the floor, neither gaining an advantage. The cop wasn't in a position to help right now.

Trezini fired and winged the escaping goon, but it was not enough to stop him. Trezini tried firing again, and discovered that he was out of bullets. In desperation – and yelling, "Josh!" – Trezini copied Delaney's move. He put his head down and charged at his goon despite the man firing again, and then grappled with him. They struggled, but Trezini soon found that his lighter frame wasn't going to prevail …

Seeing Trezini's situation, Delaney found the wherewithal to deal the hood below him a solid blow, at last dazing the man enough to take him out of the equation.

There was no clear shot to be had at the hood wrestling with Trezini, so Delaney strode closer and held his gun point-blank at the man's head. He ordered, "Let him go."

The hood reluctantly did so, lifting his hands in surrender.

Delaney and Trezini began backing away together towards the door,

Delaney holding his gun firmly aimed at the hood.

But the hood, of course, did not want to be left in the freezer – as Delaney and Trezini reached the door, the man broke his stance and rushed towards them – Delaney fired, and the hood fell.

The ordeal was over, for now at least. Delaney and Trezini turned, and headed out of the freezer as fast as they could, closing the door behind them. As it sealed, the door made a very satisfying thud.

They were lucky enough not to meet up with any other hoods or mobsters. Neither Delaney nor Trezini were in any condition to do anything more than leave as quickly and surreptitiously as possible, so they walked down a corridor or two until they saw an external door, maintaining a wary watch for trouble. The pair were slowly beginning to warm up, though both men moved with difficulty and the slimmer Trezini was still in obvious discomfort.

As they drew near the door, Trezini spoke quietly. "I don't want to hear any more foolish offers of redemption."

A moment passed before Delaney gave a reluctant nod. He didn't lift his head to meet Trezini's open expression.

"And," the man continued, "you don't want me kissing you again."

Another nod.

They had reached the door now. Both men hesitated. At last, the mobster offered to shake hands, and the cop did so. Delaney felt a little better for the gesture, though there was an undeniable sense of business unresolved.

Despite his greater need for it, Trezini shrugged off Delaney's coat, and gave it back. "Goodbye, Officer Delaney," Trezini said.

Delaney found himself staring at this strange and rather compelling man. But then he recalled himself and his situation – he pushed open the door. Both Trezini and Delaney looked carefully around, and saw that there was no one to hinder them leaving. And then they parted company with nary a backwards glance.

CHAPTER TWO

It was some while before Delaney found a mug-shot of Carmine Angelo Trezini. He stared at it long enough to soak up the detail, and then turned the page.

Delaney was sitting in his supervisor's tiny office, wrapped up in a blanket, drinking too much coffee, and feeling rather tired and dispirited. Although it was late at night – actually, very early in the morning – the squad room was bustling with activity, and the thin office walls did little to shield him from the impatient dealings between the cops and their suspects. Everything was dully lit, so Delaney had been frowning in concentration as he scanned through the folders of mug-shots. Now that he'd found who he'd been looking for, Delaney needed only to glance through the rest, though he was careful not to make it obvious to anyone else that he really wasn't trying anymore.

Trezini's mug-shot had been taken years ago, when his hairline was high rather than receding, and his features were noticeably more youthful. One thing hadn't changed, though, and that was his expression of distant arrogance; his manner had been exactly the same when Delaney first met him that night. To Delaney's surprise, that arrogance had proved to be more than simple bravado. It seemed that, subconsciously at least, Trezini knew his life was privileged, even though on the surface he was all brash attitude. Delaney wondered how many people underestimated or misjudged this man.

The mobster's manner had soon changed once the two men had begun talking. People rarely confided in Delaney – when it finally happened, the fact that it was a mobster with a regretful conscience only made the situation feel even more unlikely.

No, it had been real enough. Trezini had been spontaneous, honest. He'd thought they would die, but his confession hadn't seemed to be a last minute bid for absolution. Not that Delaney really knew how all that worked for someone who was presumably Catholic. But if Trezini's regrets were designed only to earn him a place in heaven, then surely the man would have seized Delaney's offer of working with him against Matthew Picano, knowing that he would die before being required to act on any promises. Was that too cynical an assumption? Anyway, Trezini had instead dismissed the idea out of hand, for being too dangerous. Surely the man had been genuine …

"What are you puzzling over?"

It was Lieutenant Christine Eliot, Delaney's boss. Having walked into her office with her usual businesslike stride, she pushed the door closed and then came over to stand near Delaney. Her arms were crossed and her manner was abrupt – but she was too short to give the effect of looming over him, despite that he was sitting down and therefore had to look up at her. Delaney shook his head to indicate the puzzle wasn't anything of significance, and turned another page.

Eliot continued, "Okay, the team's left for the warehouse, just in case anyone was stupid enough to hang around." She gestured at the folder of mug-shots. "Find anything there?"

"No, ma'am," Delaney replied. "I don't know who he was."

"Well, you've done enough for tonight. I don't want to hear any more protests – I'm taking you down to the hospital to get checked out."

Delaney shrugged. By now, he was too tired to care very much. Eliot took the folder out of his hands, he managed to stand without assistance, and then, still wrapped in the blanket, Delaney let his boss escort him out through the squad room.

Trezini was wearier than he ever remembered being. He hadn't slept; instead he had lain awake in a cocoon of quilts, trying to get warm again, and endeavoring to fathom his own motivations. What on earth had possessed him to speak so frankly to a cop? So, Officer Joshua Delaney was handsomer and more decent than anyone had any right to be – but that didn't change the fact that he was too dumb and too harmless for Trezini to have made such a fool of himself over.

Although, for a harmless hunk, Delaney had said some alarming things. Stupid things. *You could still become the man you wanted to be …* Damn him!

"Who was the cop? One of ours?"

Trezini shook himself and sat up straighter in his chair. Matthew Picano had spoken, and Trezini had committed the unpardonable sin of not paying attention. "I'm sorry?" Trezini murmured, casting a look around his colleagues in Picano's inner circle.

"Are you okay, Cat?" Picano asked, standing over him and apparently feeling secure enough to indulge Trezini with a concerned smile.

"Sure, I'll be fine." Trezini's memory belatedly prompted him on Picano's question. "Oh, who was the cop? I didn't know him. We barely spoke. We were both just trudging around in our little circles, trying to stay warm." Trezini mimed this by walking two fingers around on Matthew's desk, then capped the performance off with an exaggerated shiver.

The other five guys had already been entertained by Trezini's story of the absurd situation he'd found himself in – they dutifully reprised their laughter now, while Picano remained coolly amused.

Trezini lifted his chin in acknowledgement, and returned to business. "We cooperated long enough to get out of there, then we went our separate ways."

"You each shot one of Smith's men," Picano said with a hint of severity.

Trezini shrugged. "Didn't have much choice. Is that going to cause trouble?"

Picano stepped back, propped his rear on his desk, and surveyed the six men sitting in a loose semicircle before him: their boss was about to announce his view of the world. "Yes, that's going to cause trouble. But they had the nerve to put my man in a damned freezer. And they started it when they tried to buck me." Picano met Trezini's gaze. "You popping one of their men, Cat – well, there's hurt on both sides. That helps me put a lid on this real quick, as long as Smith swears fidelity. And *means* it this time."

There was a thoughtful pause, which no one dared interrupt.

Trezini took the opportunity to consider this man he'd known all his life. Although Picano always ran these inner-circle meetings in a calm and casual manner, there was something about him that ensured everyone knew he was in charge. Perhaps Matthew had been born with more than his fair share of charisma, or perhaps his easy self-assurance was the result of growing up knowing that he was his father's son and heir. He certainly presented himself to advantage; always handsome and well-groomed, today Matthew was dressed in a suit that cost more than most people earned in a month.

Picano and Trezini were the same age. Together, they'd gone through school; together, they'd played football with far more enthusiasm than ability. Sometimes it was difficult to reconcile the memory of a boyish Matthew bouncing around celebrating someone else scoring their team's touchdown, covered in mud and grinning like the most delightful of maniacs

– it was hard to fit that memory with the current image of a successful and powerful man, answerable to no one, standing here giving orders in his richly furnished and staggeringly well-equipped home office.

"Genari," Picano was saying to one of the others, "I want you to talk to our boys in blue. Be tactful, but see how far they're going to push this. I need to know if we have to put a lid on that, too."

"Sure, Mr. Picano," Genari responded.

None of the others were quite as refined as Picano or Trezini, though they all looked far more like businessmen than hoods. And that was how the mob worked these days.

Picano's body language relaxed again, his manner becoming less serious, indicating that he was now preparing to wind up the meeting. "The worst of it is," he commented to Trezini, "you lost another of your nine lives."

"How many lives are you down to, Trez?" one of the others asked.

Trezini brushed this off easily. "Oh, don't you worry, I've still got a few left."

"Anything else?" Picano asked, looking around. Apparently not. "Okay," he said, "back to work, then!"

The other five guys filed out. Trezini stayed behind, as he usually did after their regular meetings, for a few moments alone with Picano.

Forever busy, the man had already begun sorting through paperwork on his desk. Distracted by business, Picano nevertheless asked, "*Are* you all right? God, getting trapped in a freezer … I want you to know I won't let them get away with it – or, if I need to, you understand I'm not taking it lightly."

Trezini couldn't find it in him to care right now. "Just do what you have to do, Matt."

Picano continued in chatty, confiding tones, "It's good that we don't have an investment in the cop. Just between you and me, Smith is going to have the guy taken out. Ties up a loose end, and gives young Tony a chance to get his feet wet." Glancing across at Trezini, Picano offered, "So that's one less witness for you to worry about, okay?"

For his boss's benefit, Trezini managed to nod vague acceptance of this news. However, as Picano's concentration returned to his paperwork, Trezini sank further into his chair, brought low by some emotion he couldn't quite name. What was this sadness pouring through him, this ache of loss?

Grief, perhaps? Trezini hadn't felt grief since his father's funeral, and even then it had been complicated by other things: frustration, regret, resentment. Matters left unsaid and undone. There was regret mixed in with the grief now, too.

Trezini was sorry that the beautiful man he'd kissed last night was going to die. He was sorry the cop who'd seemed to know more about honor and respect than any mobster was going to be tidied out of the way. But that was the price some people paid for living in this place. Delaney should never have come to Chicago.

I believe that redemption is the stuff of life … A fitting epitaph for Joshua Delaney's lost soul.

The trouble was that Trezini knew a tiny part of him was sorry for one thing more – he was sorry he hadn't had the courage to believe, in the way that Delaney believed, not even for that brief stretch of time he was being held in the man's arms. Redemption. It was impossible, of course. But it would have been nice to take the opportunity to dream about it, just for those few moments.

What to do? How to ease this grief within him, how to reconcile his wayward regret?

Without conscious thought, Trezini had turned to his church. He was kneeling there now, alone in the shadows of the front pew, praying. Where was the strength and guidance he needed? He hadn't felt this confused since he was a teenager.

Conflicting impulses warred within him. Here, in the West Side of Chicago, there could be no half measures; yet a full measure of redemption was impossible. What to do, what to do, how to live with this, how to let Joshua Delaney die?

Still horribly unsure but unable to remain longer in the heart of his turmoil, Trezini began to return to reason. Sanity. There was nothing he *could* do. Was there? When he tried to stand, his legs and back felt like those of an old man. And his hands were numb – he looked down to see that his wooden rosary beads had left cruel indentations in his flesh.

He noticed that the priest was hovering uncertainly at the door to the sacristy, warily watching Trezini. Perhaps he'd been there all along, troubled by Trezini's prayers. Who knew what awful and desperate deeds the religious feared the mobster would do once Trezini left the church?

Trezini hardly knew himself.

Midnight, and Delaney's shift had just ended. He accompanied his partner down the sidewalk towards Watson's car. They were both silent, Watson having finally managed to reach the end of his complaints about a police officer who was stupid enough to let himself get locked in a walk-in freezer by a group of low-level wiseguys. Delaney lifted a hand in farewell as Watson climbed into his car and drove off.

Alone again, Delaney walked on, lost in contemplating all that had happened in the past twenty-four hours, and sadly considering opportunities missed. It was a great pity that Angelo Trezini hadn't wanted to take up Delaney's offer; that the cop hadn't been able to persuade the mobster to act on his conscience. The world was poorer for it.

As for Trezini's romantic – well, as for his *sexual* approaches, Delaney still didn't know quite what to make of the matter. He'd been kissed by a man, and he had no idea what to do with that fact. He had little experience with kisses, for a start, and it was a very long time since he'd had expectations of gaining more – on top of which, he'd never quite envisaged someone as unconventional as Angelo Trezini being interested in him.

He turned down a familiar street, absently noting that the night was darker than usual. A couple of the street-lamps were broken. Everything was dim and hushed, and that suited Delaney's mood. He wasn't expecting trouble.

Halfway down the street Delaney walked under the straggling branches of a struggling tree – and was more startled than hurt by a heavy impact across his shoulders. He sank to his knees, momentarily unable to take a breath.

There were four young men, all carrying baseball bats. Delaney was surrounded before he had time to think. And his ambushers weren't afraid to act on their advantage – they hit Delaney enough times with the bats to quickly render him half-unconscious and virtually immobile. Even so, his instinct was not to draw his gun. Delaney didn't want to kill any of these youths, not unless he really had to, and the threat might only provoke them to do something even more drastic.

For now, they were content with overpowering him, which seemed to indicate they were only interested in robbing him. Once Delaney was lying there on the broken concrete of the sidewalk, too dazed and hurt to do anything, the young men quit hitting him and began a hurried conference. While Delaney couldn't make out exactly what they were talking about, he noted that the four of them were betraying some inexperience and lack of confidence.

Within moments, however, a decision was made. One of them tied Delaney's hands in front of him, and then they clumsily picked him up and began carrying him across the street.

This wasn't good. Delaney mumbled some pathetic kind of plea for reason to prevail, but they easily ignored him. He was bundled into the trunk of a car, slammed into confinement and darkness. His fresh bruises were already beginning to ache, and the only thing he could count as lucky was that he seemed to have avoided suffering any broken bones.

Kidnapping – but why? Delaney assumed this had something to do with unwittingly stumbling into trouble on the previous night; anything else would be too big a coincidence. So where was he being taken? Who wanted to do what to him, and why?

This wasn't a good situation at all.

Trezini was sitting in his car, parked almost out of sight in a cross-street. Young Tony didn't realize he'd been followed here, didn't realize Trezini had witnessed the ambush of Officer Delaney. Trezini watched now as Tony shook hands with his three friends, who then headed off down the street, moving fast and high on adrenalin. Tony had to do the rest on his own, that was how this kind of thing worked. The young man climbed into his car – the car with a cop in its trunk – and drove off.

Even though Tony seemed safely oblivious, Trezini waited until the guy's car reached the next cross-street and signaled a turn before he switched on his lights and pulled away from the curb. For a wannabe mobster, Tony was way too easy to keep track of.

Tony had chosen a relatively good location for murder, however. When Trezini carefully eased a door open and peered in through the gap, he saw Tony's car parked in the middle of an abandoned warehouse. There was no one around in this block or the next at this time of night, and if Tony was smart enough to use a silencer then it was unlikely anyone would be any the wiser. The body could be left here or dumped somewhere else.

It was obvious that the young man was nervous. Tony was pacing up and down beside the car, gun grasped in one jittery hand, apparently trying to psych himself up to do this deed. Trezini wasn't too late.

Startled at hearing a door being firmly closed, Tony spun around so quickly he almost fell. But the young man was swamped by relief once he recognized the intruder. "Trez! Thank God, am I glad to see you."

Trezini walked towards him, calm and in complete control. He said, "I can't let you do this, Tone."

"It's all right," Tony reassured him with boyish earnestness, "Mr. Smith told me to. He said Mr. Picano agreed, he said they'd look after me."

"And I'm telling you, don't do it."

Trezini had reached Tony's side by now. The young man was staring at him blankly, focused only on getting this done. Tony explained, "But I want to do it, I want to get made, Trez; you understand." It finally occurred to him to ask, "Hey, did Mr. Picano send you?"

There was only one way out of this. Trezini sighed. And then he gently pried Tony's gun from his hands. The young man didn't resist, unaware of any reason why he shouldn't trust this long-familiar face. Trezini murmured, "No, Matthew didn't send me."

And Trezini lifted the gun to Tony's heart, and fired.

It was as clean and quick as possible; Tony would have hardly realized what was happening. Trezini stood there, contemplating the results of what he'd done. He didn't want to waste time with false remorse, but it was important for a man to acknowledge his own actions. Perhaps he offered up a brief prayer.

A long moment later, Trezini raised his head, and slipped the gun into his pocket. He'd need to discard the evidence somewhere safe, but that could wait.

Using a handkerchief to prevent leaving fingerprints, Trezini took the car keys from the ignition, and opened the trunk. There was Delaney, bundled up and in great discomfort. Despite the cop not knowing who to expect when the trunk opened, Delaney's face didn't betray any surprise or fear or relief.

Trezini silently helped Delaney clamber out, and then untied his wrists.

The man was moving stiffly, obviously in pain. There was blood on his hands and wrists, and dry trickles of it ran down from his temple and his mouth. Delaney insisted on taking the two steps necessary for him to see the body lying by the side of the car. The two men gazed down at what remained on this earth of young Tony.

"Don't thank me," Trezini finally said, "or I'll do you as well."

Delaney's calm melted away and he responded to Trezini's bitterness with compassion. That handsome face had never appeared more open to Trezini, not even while Delaney was offering him redemption.

Worried that the man didn't have the stamina or the balance to stand on his own two feet, Trezini was holding him with both arms around Delaney's waist. A moment passed by as they searched each other's gazes and began to realize that the connection between them was in fact mutual, that the regret over parting ways was shared.

Trezini gradually tightened his embrace, slowly bent his head closer, giving the man the chance to protest. But Delaney seemed to be simply waiting. Their mouths met, and the stillness resounded between them.

This time, Delaney cooperated when Trezini at last began kissing him.

"Come home with me," Trezini had insisted. "I'm not letting you out of my sight. At least," he'd added with a small unreadable smile, "not just yet."

Delaney had tried to demur, but could think of no real grounds on which to protest, and so was helped out of the warehouse and into Trezini's car – which was as understated and expensive as the man's clothes. Neither man spoke during the journey, and Trezini in particular seemed lost in thought. They had left the young man's body undisturbed beside his car.

Within fifteen minutes, Trezini was pulling up beside a large old home in a comfortably well-off West Side neighborhood. Beckoning once, Trezini led Delaney around to the back of the house, through an external door and into the kitchen.

A light had been left on, and Trezini apparently expected to see someone there but the room was empty. As Trezini hung up his coat and helped Delaney off with his, the cop took the opportunity to look around. The house gave an impression of shabbiness that was at odds with Trezini's personal style, but he obviously belonged here; perhaps he'd walked in through that door every day of his life.

"Are you hungry?" Trezini murmured. His manner was quiet, as if he assumed there was someone asleep in the house.

Unwisely, Delaney shook his head – and couldn't repress a wince as the ache that had been hovering round his skull now settled in for the duration. "No."

Trezini smiled wryly at him, and turned away to rummage through one of the higher cabinets. Within moments a glass of water and two aspirin were pressed into Delaney's hands. "Well, I'm starving," Trezini said, "and I think you should eat."

Once the water and pain-killers hit his stomach, Delaney was inclined to agree. Before he had time to reply, though, and before Trezini had done much more than peer into the fridge, a woman entered the kitchen from elsewhere in the house. She was dressed for bed and her demeanor indicated that she had been woken from a doze. An expression of relief at seeing Trezini slowly turned to wariness as she absorbed the fact that a uniformed police officer was standing in her kitchen.

Trezini immediately went to her, walking around the table in the center of the room – and the man managed to envelop her in a hug, despite the fact that she was over twice his width. He bent his head to press a kiss to her hair. "Home at last, Ma," Trezini said. "Sorry, did you wait up for me? I had to rescue Josh here from a bit of trouble."

"Trouble?" The woman gazed up at her son, hands patting at his face and shoulders as if to reassure herself that he was whole. "Are you hurt, Angelo?"

"No, I'm fine." And the man gently detached himself. "Ma, is there any soup or something you could heat up? I haven't eaten all day."

"Of course. There's the minestrone I made this afternoon."

Trezini gave her a broad smile. "Perfect." Indicating Delaney, he said, "Ma, this is Joshua Delaney. He was stuck in that freezer with me last night, and he saved my life; it was only fair that I return the favor."

"Pleased to meet you, ma'am," Delaney offered.

The woman nodded an acknowledgement of his greeting, her face troubled. It obviously made even less sense to her than to Delaney himself, that her son the mobster should bring a police officer home with him. However, she took refuge in the ordinary and began preparing a meal for the two men, lighting the stove and shifting a large pot onto the blue flames.

"Now," Trezini said, sounding supremely satisfied, "let's take care of you, Josh."

Despite a protest that he was all right, Delaney was pushed down to sit on a chair at the kitchen table. Trezini reached for a first aid kit from the same cabinet he'd taken the aspirin from, and brought it over to Delaney. Carefully though briskly, Trezini cleaned the blood away from Delaney's face, and then pressed a piece of sticking plaster over a cut on his temple. It seemed to the cop, who was required to keep his first aid certificate current, that Trezini hadn't been formally trained – but it was also apparent that the mobster had dealt with injuries before.

Kneeling on the floor in front of Delaney, Trezini worked on cleaning Delaney's wrists. The skin was raw from his struggles against the ropes that bound him; Trezini soothed some antiseptic cream into the slight injuries.

Then the mobster sat back on his heels and cast an assessing glance over the cop. "You'll be all right," Trezini said. "Though I'm glad those morons had no idea what they were doing."

"Unfortunately," Delaney responded, "they were learning fast."

Trezini smiled up at him, apparently liking Delaney's sense of humor. Without turning his gaze away from Delaney, Trezini announced, "Ma, I have to tell you that I'm in love with this man. We saved each other's lives once or twice, and I fell in love with him."

Delaney was mortified by this bluntness. There was a fraught silence, and the cop closed his eyes for a moment. Then, endeavoring not to die of embarrassment, Delaney turned to look over at the mobster's mother to see how she was taking this.

Well, it seemed that Trezini's homosexuality wasn't news to her – though, naturally enough, she had other problems with the potential relationship. "He's a police officer, Angelo."

Trezini reached to run a fond caress over Delaney's hair. "Falling for Josh is the smartest thing I've ever done."

"Matthew Picano won't think so." It seemed that the woman was as blunt as her son.

Standing, Trezini left Delaney and walked over to hug his mother again, hampering her efforts at preparing bread to accompany the soup. "No, he won't like it," Trezini agreed. In gentle tones he continued, "Josh and me, we're going to work together to put Matt out of business. We're going to bring Matthew to justice, Ma."

The woman was shocked to a halt. "*No, Angelo.*"

"Be happy for me," Trezini murmured, "be proud of me. I'm going to do some good."

"But you know what will happen!"

Delaney said firmly, "Of course there will be some danger involved, ma'am, but I will –"

For the first time, she spoke to him directly – interrupting Delaney to cry out, *"They'll kill him!"* And she could see that hit home so hard he felt winded. She turned back to her son. "Angelo, you know this! What are you doing?"

Trezini said, "I'm sorry, but I need to do this no matter how much it hurts."

The woman was crying. Trezini gathered her closer into the most comforting and unconditional of hugs; Delaney watched them, caught off balance by the intimacy the man was displaying in this most difficult of moments. Angelo Trezini had completely opened himself to his mother's grief, despite the fact that he was the one causing it. This generous openness, this utter vulnerability was evident in every comforting line of Trezini's body, every expression of his face soaking in the woman's sorrow. Unexpectedly, Delaney found himself reflecting that to be loved by this man might be something incredible.

Unable to remain silent, Delaney said to the woman, "I promise you I will do everything in my power to ensure that Angelo remains safe."

However, it soon became obvious that this did not reassure anyone other than Delaney himself. Trezini loosened his embrace a little, turned his unguarded face to Delaney, and said very calmly, "Matthew will have his revenge, Josh. That's a fact. We just need to do as much good as we can before he ends it."

"Ends it?" Delaney echoed in a whisper.

"He'll kill me," the man said flatly. "No matter what we do, no matter how clever we are, he'll get to me. Don't tell me you didn't know that."

But he hadn't known that. Delaney sat back in his chair, staggered by the implications, finally realizing the extent of the danger. How stupid had he been? He was afraid that the answer was *'very* stupid'. "I'll do everything I can," he repeated lamely. And until now, Delaney had assumed that would be enough. He and Trezini had survived everything that had occurred during the past twenty-four hours, after all – but of course that was no guarantee they'd survive working directly against Matthew Picano.

His tone easy now that his point had been made, Trezini was saying to his mother, "How's that soup coming?"

Despite her own state of shock, the woman served up the soup and bread for the two men. Trezini sat beside Delaney at the table and ate hungrily, while Delaney had to force himself to swallow a few mouthfuls, knowing that he should eat even though he had no taste for it. Trezini's mother was making herself busy, cleaning the kitchen and setting it to rights. She was still weeping.

The two of them weren't exaggerating about Trezini's likely fate, or at least not to any significant degree. And Delaney couldn't help but recall that he had gotten Trezini into this: the cop had been the one with the bright idea of working against Picano; the mobster had at first been smart enough to turn him down, dismissing the notion out of hand. What on earth had persuaded him to do otherwise?

As his mother was helping him to a second serving of soup, Trezini murmured, "Ma, we're all going to have to be strong for a while because I need to do this. Can you let me do this?"

"I don't want to lose you, Angelo."

Trezini said, "Josh is giving me the chance of redemption and I love him for it, and nothing's more important than that."

"Redemption?" The woman was staring fiercely at her son now, drawing strength from the word. She asked, "Is God calling you?"

"Yes, Ma. God's calling me."

"Then … you must do what God tells you to do, and I'll pray for you."

Trezini smiled at her, and lowered his head again to finish his soup.

Delaney could see it clearly when someone else was on the receiving end of Trezini's heartfelt conviction: it was impossible to argue against him when he started wielding the most fundamental of abstract nouns. *Love. Redemption. Faith.* And when Trezini was so obviously intent on doing good, it was almost as impossible to mind being manipulated.

This was – wasn't it? – how the world should be.

Once Trezini had finished his meal, he stood, and took the empty bowl over to his mother; as she took it from him, he gave her a kiss. And Trezini announced, "Josh is staying over tonight, all right?"

Delaney knew that his face paled; he was vastly uncomfortable with this aspect of his strange new relationship with Angelo Trezini. The man's mother cast a glare in Delaney's direction, no doubt unwilling to welcome him further into her home. But apparently she felt as little able to argue with Trezini right now as Delaney did.

"Come upstairs," Trezini was saying to Delaney; "have a shower at least. There's a guest bedroom if you're going to get coy on me."

He didn't have the words to respond – and even if he had, Delaney's breath was caught in his throat, stopping his voice.

Trezini's expression softened a little, though his determination didn't. "Look," the man said, "if you already had someone in your life, you'd have mentioned that by now. Wouldn't you?"

Delaney was forced to acknowledge the truth of this with a small nod.

"And it's not like you haven't kissed me back once or twice …"

Knowing that embarrassment was adding heat and color to his cheeks, Delaney tried to rationally consider the invitation. But he felt there was little he could do but agree – at least on the basis that the guest bedroom was available. After all, he and Trezini really should talk further about the Picano matter, before the mobster became too committed to his wish for redemption. So, at last Delaney nodded again. "Yes," he managed. "I'll stay."

A satisfied smile relaxed Trezini's face. He said, "Goodnight, Ma," and then the man walked over, took Delaney by the hand, and led him out of the kitchen and through into the house. Delaney was granted a last glimpse of Trezini's mother watching the pair go with great foreboding lengthening her face.

Delaney came to a decision while waiting on Trezini, who was taking the first shower. He didn't say anything, however. Instead, he spent the time mentally sorting through everything that had happened and working yet again through the more feasible courses of action. It was clear that the stakes were higher than he'd anticipated, which meant their options were severely limited.

When Trezini stepped out of the shower and began drying off, he seemed as distracted by thought as Delaney was, which made it far easier for the cop to simply strip off and begin his own shower. It wasn't as if he wasn't used to showering in male company – Delaney had done that a hundred times at various police stations. The problem lay in being aware of Trezini's declared intentions.

Trezini seemed willing not to push the point, though, and his manner was very matter-of-fact. He'd left the room for a while, and now returned as Delaney was drying himself. Dressed in a robe, Trezini had also brought a robe for Delaney to wear.

Breaking the silence, Delaney announced, "We can't proceed against Picano."

"We can and we will," Trezini said, just as firmly. "If we could do it safely or easily, someone would have already put Matt away."

Delaney stared at the man. "If you're so determined, why pick me to help you?"

Trezini cast him a dry glance. "It was tough choosing between the hundreds of cops who volunteered, so I just went with the handsomest."

Dismissing this, Delaney persisted, "You can't trust me: I've been as stupid as a rookie. I got beaten up by a bunch of kids tonight. And I should never have let them throw me in that freezer in the first place."

"But then you wouldn't have met me," Trezini replied with calm, inarguable logic.

Delaney shrugged on the robe and tied it; then Trezini took him by the hand again, and led him out of the bathroom and down the hallway. "I don't want to put your life at risk," Delaney said.

"Don't you get it? I want to do this, I want redemption, and that's what you've given me the chance for." Trezini led Delaney into another room, and closed the door behind them. In suggestive tones, Trezini added, "Of course, the love of a good man would sweeten the deal."

Made impatient by Trezini's lack of gravitas, Delaney almost let out a groan. "Angelo, please. Think of the price you might pay –"

"I've already started paying," Trezini said, interrupting. And his mood became bleaker for a moment, his face darkened; perhaps he was remembering he had killed that young man tonight for Delaney's sake. But he soon lightened again: "But I will fear no evil; For Thou art with me. Come here and kiss me, you fool."

Delaney looked around and belatedly realized they must be in Trezini's bedroom. He was unnerved all over again. "I'm really not sure I –"

"It wouldn't be our first kiss, Josh," Trezini observed in the most reasonable of tones. "And it really hasn't just been me kissing you."

"The previous ones were in rather different circumstances."

Trezini stepped closer, took Delaney's other hand in his, and spoke quietly. "I need you to wake up in my arms tomorrow morning, fully committed. I can't afford to have you getting cold feet about doing this thing with Matthew."

"I understand that," Delaney pleaded, "but this isn't something I've imagined doing before now. I'm sure you think I'm horribly conventional – but if you'd give me a little time to get used to the idea, if you could wait a day or two –" He let out a breath, feeling defeated before he'd even begun. "Angelo, I'm not even sure that I *can* right now."

"You're not going to tell me you've got a headache?" Trezini seemed amused, but there was a note of severity in his voice, too. "I know you're hurting, but I'm not expecting this to be a Super Bowl performance."

Delaney grimaced. "It's not that so much as –"

"As what? You've only been with women before – is that it?"

"Yes. Partly." How to explain, when he hardly knew himself? Delaney tried again. "Yes, but only a very few women – a long time ago – and it always seemed to go … badly wrong."

"If it's been a long time, you must be real hungry for it, at least."

"Under the circumstances, I was … happy enough to wait."

Trezini shook his head in disbelief, and then gently insisted: "Did you never wonder whether you were gay?"

A shrug rippled through Delaney's whole body, as if he were trying to physically shake off the confusion. He exclaimed, "I never really wondered whether I was anything at all!" – and then he sighed. "I'm not saying I can't be this for you. If you give me time. But I always thought, if it ever *did* come to me, it would be … quite conventional."

Trezini echoed his sigh, and mumbled, "All right, I get it. I know. The last thing I am is conventional."

The man's insistence, even his confidence, dropped away from him so completely that Delaney huffed in surprise. A moment later he was deciding to reward that with an effort of his own – he was leaning in and kissing Trezini. Unfortunately the results were clumsy and uninspired. Delaney soon drew away again, sensing nothing but failure.

"You hardly know it yet," Trezini said, beginning to weave a spell, "but you're already half in love with me. You're fascinated, and that's a good start."

Delaney tried kissing the man again – and at last they found the right rhythms. As the kiss became more impassioned, Trezini eased into Delaney's close embrace. Somehow, it seemed both strange and natural that their bodies should already be fitting together so well.

After a time Delaney broke away, and glanced towards Trezini's double bed. The bed he now knew he was going to share with this man. Scraps of Delaney's earlier mortification were still haunting him. "Forgive me," he said, "but if we could turn off the lights?"

Trezini smiled, and indulged him.

In the darkness, Delaney made his own way to the bed, settled on it, shifted towards where he knew Trezini waited. They met, and all was confusion again until their bodies rediscovered that natural fit. Their mouths answered each other's hungers, while movement became a rhythmic kaleidoscope of silk and flesh. There was the shocking intensity of male genitals pressing and shifting and jostling against his own, and Trezini murmuring his name – well, murmuring the fond, intimate, impudent name he'd given Delaney. "*Josh …*"

Trezini soon grew fraught with need, and reached completion through nothing more than this simple body-to-body caress; for a few beautiful moments, his groans conveyed the glorious feelings surging through him. And then he quieted, and lay there stretched against Delaney from head to toe, heavy with satiation.

"That was no Super Bowl performance," Trezini whispered, apparently trying to re-gather himself. "I thought I'd last the distance."

"It's all right," Delaney reassured him. "It's all right."

Trezini shifted up onto his outstretched arms, moved over him – and Delaney thought he could detect a glare aimed his way through the night's curtained dimness. No doubt he didn't appreciate being soothed.

Delaney found himself grasping the man's hips in both hands, unwilling to let him go, unsure how to gain his own goal. Unexpectedly, there was a fierce hunger burning within him; a yearning not only for his own climax, but for reaching that completion with Angelo Trezini. So much for convention! "How do I – ?" Delaney whispered, closing his eyes for a moment. "I mean, what should –"

His hands were empty now because Trezini had pulled away … but then a tongue rasped across Delaney's belly, as Trezini began licking at his own spilled seed. Delaney let out a surprised and satisfied moan – and then was reduced to a blind silent gape as Trezini took Delaney's cock into his mouth. Was this man so well practiced? Or could it be that only another man … ? Or had it simply been so very long, such a very long time since he'd –

He came with a gasp, and Trezini stayed with him, drawing out the last drops of pleasure, easing him back down again afterwards.

There were a few moments of comfortable confusion, as they discarded the robes and rearranged the bedclothes, then settled together in a companionable tangle. Delaney barely had time to wonder whether he could ever possibly fall asleep while lying in a stranger's arms before he drifted off.

Angelo Trezini woke slowly. It was early; he could tell that by the pale light and the stillness and the cool air. Trezini lay there unmoving in his disheveled bed, with a man whose hold on Trezini tightened as he also woke.

After a while, Trezini turned his head and found that Delaney was carefully watching him; perhaps the cop was surprised at where he found himself to be. The two of them gazed at each other. It would be easy to doubt everything in the dawn light, simple to pretend that no agreement had been reached the previous night. Trezini hardly knew whether he was more afraid of acting on their commitment to each other, or of backing away and returning to his familiar life.

No, he thought. Trezini could afford no more doubts. There was nothing – there must be nothing other than this pact. Making it so, Trezini murmured to his companion, "For Thou art with me."

And with barely a breath of hesitation, Delaney replied, "For Thou art with me, Angelo." Apparently wanting to seal the matter, Delaney shifted up onto an elbow, and leaned down over Trezini to kiss him.

Bless the man. When Delaney lifted his head again, Trezini smiled up at him, well-pleased. For it seemed that Joshua Delaney was exactly where Trezini wanted him to be.

CHAPTER THREE

Matthew Picano was relaxing in a comfortable chair in his office, a large wood-paneled room on the first floor of his home. He could hear laughter from the kitchen, and the shriek-and-tumble of his children playing overhead. Around his home stretched a well-tended garden, and beyond that sprawled the neighborhood he'd grown up in, every street and building and alleyway familiar. The image of a smug spider had occurred to Matthew before, and he contemplated it again, sitting here in the center of a web that covered the entire West Side, its shimmering and almost invisible tendrils reaching further still into all kinds of unexpected places.

The laughter drew closer, high heels tap-tapped across the hallway's slate floor, and then Matthew's wife Nicola appeared, holding the door open for Carmine Trezini who had his hands full carrying two mugs of coffee. It only added to Matthew's contentment that his old buddy Cat obviously felt right at home here, sharing a last murmured joke with Nicola before walking over to give one of the mugs to Matthew.

While Trezini settled himself on a nearby sofa, Matthew considered his beautiful wife. Nicola was a small woman with a neat figure, and it was apparent from every detail of her grooming and presentation that her husband was a wealthy man, which was exactly the way Matthew liked it to be. She turned her fond smile from Trezini to Matthew for a moment, and then tactfully withdrew, closing the door behind her.

Setting the coffee aside to cool, Matthew turned his attention to his companion, who was barely suppressing an 'I got lucky last night' grin. Matthew had to wonder if that's what Trezini and Nicola had been laughing about out there, if the two of them had been comparing notes. Strange that this man and Matthew's wife should get along so well, when they really had nothing in common. Except for Matthew himself.

When Trezini finally spoke, however, it was to ask, "So, how's your hostile takeover of the fight business going?"

Well, that was a topic on which Matthew held very clear opinions. "I tell you," he complained, "I have no idea why my father let the Tammaro brothers continue – they are running that business into the ground. I'm taking it under my wing just in time."

"That's good," Trezini replied.

Right now, though, Matthew had more pressing concerns. "You heard about young Tony?"

Trezini's mood sobered, which wasn't such a surprise. Matthew was all too aware that many of the younger guys – and even some of the older ones – tended to look to Trezini for guidance. If it had been anyone other than Cat, this might have felt like more of a threat. As it was, Matthew was happy enough to let Trezini take care of all the petty things that Picano's people wanted help with.

"Yeah, I heard," Trezini said at last. "Poor kid. I guess he bit off more than a mouthful."

"His friends went looking for him when he didn't meet them afterwards; at least he was smart enough to involve them. It's easy to assume that the cop did it, your man from the freezer. But, if so, he's not telling anyone. I understand that the police are as confused as the rest of us." Matthew looked over at Trezini, and let out a laugh. "Hey, where'd the smile go?"

Trezini glanced sidelong at Matthew and, apparently almost despite himself, his lips curled happily. Soon the grin was back in full force.

"That's better – you look like the proverbial cat who got the cream."

"It's been nothing but highs and lows lately." And Trezini said, "Yesterday, I met someone."

"You met someone? A man?"

Trezini shot him the most sardonic of looks, and said flatly, "Yeah, a man."

Matthew felt completely taken aback. It wasn't as if he didn't know this about Trezini, it wasn't as if *anyone* didn't know Trezini was queer, but rarely did Cat directly mention such matters. In fact, Matthew now realized he'd spent a lot of years comfortably assuming that Trezini was pretty much celibate. Endeavoring to recover from this patent foolishness, Matthew asked, "Well, who is he? What's he like?"

"He's incredible. Absolutely gorgeous. And married."

"Married?" Further confused, Matthew glanced down at his own wedding ring, and then back up at Trezini. "To a woman?"

Trezini let out a breath that might have been a chuckle – only Cat would've dared. "Yeah, he's married to a woman. I never knew you were so open-minded, to be thinking there's alternatives."

Deciding to let his old friend get away with this, Matthew grimaced. "Okay, so he's incredible, gorgeous, married and …"

"And we're going to have to sneak around behind his wife's back." Suddenly Trezini was gazing very directly at his boss. "I love him, Matt. This is *it* for me."

Something alarmingly close to jealousy burst through Matthew, and he frowned. Where had that come from? It certainly wasn't that Matthew had wanted this man for himself – he'd never even felt the slightest inclination to experiment. But Matthew had assumed, he supposed, that Cat's loyalty to him was complete. And it seemed that such an assumption was closer to flattery than fact. In jesting tones, Matthew said, "Hell, I thought I was the only man in your life."

"Not anymore," Trezini responded in easy tones.

Serious again, Matthew said, "I should meet him. Any of my people get involved, especially one of my inner circle, I need to know who with."

Trezini seemed reluctant, though surely he would have known this was coming. "Well, okay."

"You understand, it's nothing personal."

"Sure." But the man refused to meet Matthew's gaze. After a moment of thought, Trezini suggested, "We're meeting for lunch today at Cin Cin – you could happen to drop by, about one maybe, and I'll introduce you."

"Cin Cin?" Matthew repeated, perhaps overdoing the surprise in an effort to re-establish some kind of connection. "I thought you'd want to show off the bar."

It worked: Cat grinned at him. "Hey, I don't want any distractions, especially from work."

Delaney was sitting in a booth with a clear view of the restaurant's front door, waiting for Angelo Trezini to arrive. He remained calm, which didn't require much effort as he was used to maintaining a removed demeanor – though today he had to acknowledge there was an unexpected flutter of something in the pit of his stomach. Perhaps it wasn't so strange, really, that Delaney felt nervous. Indeed, when he had told his boss that morning of his intention to work against Matthew Picano, Lieutenant Eliot had been amazed by Delaney's apparent lack of fear or excitement – even more amazed than she'd been to hear his plan, which she characterized as audacious in her more generous moments, and stupid otherwise. He hadn't told her Angelo's name yet.

Angelo. Perhaps it wasn't strange that Delaney should feel nervous, for he had taken on a lover. A male lover. He hadn't allowed Eliot to catch even a hint of that fact. Delaney still wasn't quite sure what to think of it himself.

At last Trezini burst in, apparently conscious of being late, his gaze quickly settling on Delaney. As Trezini walked over at a more reasonable pace, Delaney summoned a pleasant smile for him – but Trezini did nothing more than anxiously scan him, and Delaney felt the smile slip away. This all felt too … new, too sudden and uncertain. Trezini slid into the seat opposite Delaney, and they stared at each other.

The mobster was expensively dressed again, in a well-cut suit that showed off his slim figure to advantage. It seemed that Trezini's goal was to make the most of what he was – however, his hair was cut short, rather than arranged to hide its retreat, so Trezini didn't seem inclined to pretend to be anything he wasn't. Delaney found the overall effect appealing.

In contrast, Delaney hadn't thought to make an effort, and had dressed in his usual casual clothes. When he'd arrived at Cin Cin, the waiter had looked askance at Delaney's jeans. Once Delaney had told them he was here to meet Mr. Trezini, however, he'd been welcomed in.

The still moment between them passed, and Trezini was talking fast as if to make up for lost time. "Sorry I'm throwing Matthew at you on short notice. But at least we'll know we can pull this off, before we go talk to your people. You've set that up?"

Another contrast between them: Trezini's manner was energetic, emotional; and it could feel quite daunting. Delaney took a breath before answering, "Yes, it's arranged for this afternoon." They had both leaned forward with their elbows on the table, but for the sake of further confidentiality Delaney lowered his voice to say, "I thought I'd arrest you for murdering that man, to explain your presence."

Trezini said dryly, "Which one?" Delaney recognized it as a rhetorical question, and didn't reply. Trezini continued, "I told Matt you're married, I figured that's good cover. It gives us an even better reason to be sneaking around."

The cop considered this for a moment, and nodded. In fact, the additional detail fit their plan so well that Delaney was surprised and a little chagrined that he hadn't thought of it himself.

"Well, so …" Trezini said, expression growing self-conscious as he fumbled around in a pocket, "I brought my Dad's wedding ring for you. I hope it fits."

There was nothing to say; Delaney simply held out his left hand. Trezini eventually produced a gold wedding band, and slipped it onto Delaney's third finger. Unused to wearing jewelry of any kind, Delaney found it an odd feeling, though the fit was perfect.

It was only then that Trezini seemed to become aware of the act's significance. His gaze abruptly rose to meet Delaney's, and he murmured, "Till death do us part, Josh."

Despite the potential for embarrassment, Delaney reached to take Trezini's hands in his, and tried to smile. "Something a little more cheerful?"

A broad grin painted itself across Trezini's face, as the man said in suggestive tones, "To *have* and to *hold* …"

The two of them let a happier moment grow between them as Delaney belatedly realized that he did indeed want to have and to hold this man. The flutter in his gut increased, and that smile worked itself loose despite his best efforts.

"Oh, stop it," Angelo happily complained, his fingers clutching tightly at Delaney's hands. "I'm feeling warm again. And you tried to tell me it was because we were freezing to death."

"It was!" Delaney protested.

"So what is it now? Josh, you big dumb hunk, if I ever stop falling for you –"

Trezini broke off, and looked up. Sensing someone standing over them, Delaney quickly followed his gaze, while forcing himself not to let go of Trezini's hands.

It was Matthew Picano: most people in Chicago would recognize this face. Picano presented himself as a successful businessman, young and cocksure, possessed of every asset from a handsome face to half of the West Side. Delaney wondered how many people in Chicago fooled themselves into seeing no deeper than Picano's plausible and attractive surface.

There was a woman standing beside Picano, taller than the mob boss, and tawdry where Picano was expensive: Delaney suspected this wasn't his wife; perhaps Picano had required protection, of a sort. The woman had been staring with some distaste at Trezini and Delaney; without uttering a word, she turned on her high heels and stalked off to a distant table. Apparently she was uncomfortable with alternate sexualities – at least when displayed in public.

Picano's manner was all cool friendship. "Cat. What a surprise. How are you doing?"

"Good, Matt," Trezini replied easily, "I'm doing fine. Hey, I'd like you to meet a new friend of mine. This is Joshua. Josh, this is Matthew."

Delaney rose to his feet as well as he could within the confines of the booth, and shook Picano's hand. "Pleased to meet you, Matthew."

"Likewise," the mob boss responded in a perfunctory manner. He didn't even blink when Delaney sat back down and again reached for Trezini's hands. "I thought I knew everyone on the West Side. You don't live around here?"

"No."

Picano lifted a brow, perhaps expecting a more detailed reply. "So, what do you think of our neighborhood? The natives are obviously friendly …"

Playing along, Delaney continued, "… and there's plenty of local color."

"What do you do? What's your work?"

"Well, I'm just starting out as a freelance writer," Delaney said. He and Trezini had agreed on this as part of their cover: it made Delaney virtually untraceable. "No success to speak of yet."

"Yeah? So, you work from home, your time's your own. That must make you quite … flexible."

Trezini's expression had been darkening and he interrupted to ask, "Matthew, what's with the interrogation?"

Picano ignored this, and said abruptly to Delaney, "Carmine Trezini is a friend of mine. And friends mean something around here."

"Matt, come on!" Trezini protested.

"He's a friend of mine, too, Matthew," Delaney smoothly replied.

"So we understand each other?"

"Yes, I believe so."

"Good," Picano said, dropping the severe tones as if Trezini was only a minor detail after all. "I'll see you at the bar tonight, Cat." And Picano walked off to join his companion at their table on the far side of the restaurant.

Trezini sagged, and let his head rest against the back of his seat. "Oh God."

Despite continuing to feel uneasy at this display of affection, Delaney didn't let the man's hands go until Trezini indicated he'd recovered his composure. Perhaps Delaney had been unforgivably slow, but it was only now that the cop began to realize how personal a loyalty the mobster was betraying. What on earth had Delaney gotten Trezini into?

Delaney had left Trezini sitting at his desk in the squad room; the mobster was wearing handcuffs and a studiously nonchalant manner. Unfortunately, the squad room was even busier than usual, crammed full of cops and suspects, and it seemed that every last one of them knew who Trezini was. Stares of hostility and curiosity were leveled at him – especially by Robert Watson, Delaney's partner, who was of course sitting at the next desk along.

Although he disliked leaving Trezini alone out there, Delaney had been summoned by Lieutenant Eliot and there was no disobeying her when she was in this kind of mood. The two of them were standing in Eliot's office with the door closed and Delaney was paying strict attention to her tirade, though he deliberately kept Trezini in his line of sight.

"Do you really have a grasp on the size of this thing?" Eliot was asking. Although she was keeping her voice low to avoid everyone else hearing, this only added venom to her delivery. "I just don't get how one day you're fretting over the number of outstanding parking tickets in the city, and the next you're wanting to take down the biggest mob boss in Chicago. How do you make that kind of leap?"

"Well," Delaney began, "I met Mr. Trezini –"

"– in a walk-in freezer of all places," Eliot supplied.

"And when I understood something of the kind of man he is –"

Eliot interrupted him. "Trezini is a two-bit hood with an ounce of flash. Tell me," she pleaded, "you don't find him so impressive in the cold light of day." Then it was back to the venom: "And, by the way, so much for you not knowing who he was that night."

Delaney declared, "Mr. Trezini is a man with an ethical heart, and he's risking his life just being here, ma'am. I find that impressive."

"You actually think he wants to turn on Picano? You're day-dreaming." Eliot tried the reasonable approach: "Joshua, you don't understand the strength of the loyalties between these people. Those two grew up together."

The phone rang, and Eliot grimaced with impatience as she picked up the receiver. "Lieutenant Eliot, thirty-third."

Delaney could just make out the message: "The state attorney and the FBI agent are both here, ma'am."

"Good. Thanks," Eliot responded. She hung up the phone and looked very directly up at Delaney. "You need to convince these people," she told him. "And try not to embarrass us – I feel like an idiot for even calling them."

"Yes, ma'am," Delaney said.

"You didn't tell me the whole story this morning."

"No, ma'am. I didn't feel I was in a position to do so."

Eliot's gaze narrowed; she didn't bother asking whether she knew the full story now. A long moment stretched – and then at last, still unappeased, Eliot led the way out of her office.

Delaney quickly headed over to collect Trezini and escort him to the interview rooms. Things were going about as well as could be expected, he supposed. That only proved once more that Trezini knew what he was talking about: *If we could do it safely or easily, someone would have already put Matt away.* This wasn't going to be as straightforward as Delaney had initially thought.

Tensions continued to run high. Delaney was sitting on one side of an inordinately large table, with Eliot at his right and Trezini on his left. The three of them were facing Deputy Prosecuting Attorney Denise Valeri and FBI Special Agent Edgar Russell. Trezini was uncuffed now, though his manner remained distant. The others were all suffering through varying degrees of earnest frustration. The room itself didn't help: the atmosphere was steeped in decades of use and abuse.

"No, sir," Delaney was saying to the FBI Agent, "but I have over twelve years' experience in local law enforcement, mainly in rural areas –"

Russell couldn't resist interrupting him: "And I have almost twenty years' service with the Federal Bureau of Investigation, so I know what I'm talking about when I tell you that you have no idea what you're doing."

Delaney asked very levelly, "Are you saying it's impossible to bring Matthew Picano to justice?"

"Well," Russell replied, sitting back a little. His face and body and general presentation seemed as world-weary as his attitude. "Let's just say that he and his family, and a whole lot of people like them, have been an intrinsic part of Chicago for decades."

"Mr. Trezini is giving us a chance to change that."

Valeri spoke up. She was a comfortably large woman, professionally dressed, whose habitual expression seemed to be one of thoughtful consideration. "Don't get me wrong, Officer Delaney – it's tempting to try. Hell, everyone I work with came out of law school dreaming of prosecuting Picano or his father. But, realistically, how far would we get?"

"I was expecting more enthusiasm," Delaney said. "Not to mention respect for the position Mr. Trezini has put himself in."

Surprisingly enough, Christine Eliot's anger seemed to have been drained away by this opposition. With some sympathy she said to Delaney, "Just because you're the fools wanting to rush in, doesn't mean the rest of us are keen to follow you."

Angelo Trezini hadn't said a word so far. Perhaps he was moved to do so now because Delaney wasn't making any progress. "You know who I am?" Trezini demanded.

"Sure," Russell replied. "One of Picano's hangers-on. We have a file."

"Then you should know better than to underestimate me. As for dismissing Officer Delaney's intentions –"

Valeri offered, "I'm interested, Mr. Trezini, but Picano's a clever man – you'd know that better than we do – he keeps everything at a distance."

"Except me," Trezini countered.

Russell grunted his disbelief. "And what are you – his confidante? His best buddy?"

"He's not the confiding type, but I'm as close as you'll get." On the attack again, Trezini declared, "All we need you to do is what you're paid for. All we're asking is that you do what you're *sworn* to do."

Not taking kindly to this, Russell said, "Back off with the attitude, Trezini."

"Yes, Officer Delaney is naive," Trezini continued regardless. He got to his feet, the better to deal with his own energy. "But maybe that's what it takes to see that Matthew Picano doesn't have to be intrinsic to Chicago after all."

"You should take this show on the road and convert the masses."

"Yeah, let's not shy away from that idea. This man and I have the faith and the motivation – you lot should just do your damned jobs. And you might be amazed to discover that miracles can happen."

Delaney just sat there, carefully not gaping. He was all too aware that the mobster had already converted the cop, with Trezini's passion and his unexpected yearning for redemption. How could the others remain so unimpressed?

Apparently the attorney was halfway converted, for she said, "I really wish we could, Mr. Trezini, but –"

"– but we're doing this," Trezini announced. "We've already got the cover set up."

Russell looked furious. "Aren't you getting about a hundred miles ahead of yourself?"

Unfazed, Trezini continued, "I'll tell you how it's going to happen. I figure you need information. You need to interview me, you need to build up a case."

"Yes," Valeri tentatively agreed.

"But it's going to take a while, and I want to live what's left of my life. So, Picano thinks I'm having a fling with a married man. Three afternoons a week, I rock up to a cheap hotel, and Officer Delaney drags me inside in a passionate embrace. You people set up for the interviews in an adjoining room."

The others were all rather taken aback. Delaney couldn't tell what surprised them most: the detailed plans or the homosexual angle.

Eliot was frowning, trying to keep up. "What will – Well. Will Picano buy that story about an affair? With a man?"

"Sure," Trezini said easily. "Picano wanted to meet him, but that went all right."

This announcement caused some consternation. Eliot turned to her subordinate and dazedly asked, "You *met* him – ?"

Delaney explained, "I was having lunch with Mr. Trezini today, so when Mr. Picano insisted on being introduced, it seemed easiest to –"

"God, I'd suspend you if I weren't getting intrigued. You're presenting us with a *fait accompli*."

"That wasn't my intention, ma'am."

Valeri was puzzling over the details. "What could we manage? Two hours at a time?"

Trezini replied, "Two hours is fine. That means I get one hour alone with Officer Delaney, then you get one hour for the interviews."

"What's the hour with Delaney for?" Valeri asked. "He's really not qualified to participate in the interview process."

The mobster was laughing to himself, which left the cop to announce, "Mr. Trezini and I have actually commenced a relationship."

"A relationship?" Eliot repeated blankly.

Delaney turned to her, endeavoring not to blush and failing miserably. "An affair, ma'am."

Of course, this announcement caused even more consternation.

Russell looked absolutely disgusted. "Oh, don't tell me – you two got the hots for each other and decided this crusade against Picano was the only way you could be together."

"Delaney," Eliot protested, "you're the straightest guy I ever worked with."

"No, I, uh –" He started again. "It seems that … appearances can be deceptive, ma'am."

"No way can we do this," Russell was saying. He sagged in his seat, and rubbed at his face with both hands as if trying to wake up. "*Christ,* what a mess."

Trezini said, "It's not a mess, it's the perfect cover. It gives me a reason to be sneaking around. Matthew always knew I'm gay – one look at Delaney, it's obvious what the attractions are – Picano's just going to let me get on with it."

Russell let out a bitter laugh. "No, what it does is ruin your credibility as a witness. It turns the whole scenario into a farce."

"My *credibility*? God, drag yourself into the nineties. Give me any jury, they'll buy me." Trezini threw a gesture at Valeri: "Let her select the *right* jury, they'll all want to take us home with them."

"One hour of queer sex with a cop," Russell muttered, still deep in his nightmare, "on the federal budget no doubt, and one hour of spilling your guts."

"Fuck your budget," Trezini carelessly replied. "I'll pay for my own damned hotel room."

Russell glared up at him, and turned nasty. "This isn't some fury-of-a-man-scorned thing, is it?"

"No." Trezini's tone was just as firm, but his manner was more reasonable. "And it's not about Picano, it's about me."

"It's a farce!"

A silence lengthened. Eliot, Valeri and Delaney exchanged glances, none of them quite sure how best to cut through this animosity.

At last Trezini stepped forward and rested both hands on the table, leaning towards Russell. He said with quiet sincerity, "This crusade is something I have to do. And I'll be dead by the end of it, if not sooner." He stood up again, wryness stretching his lips into something like a smile. "But the ironic thing is, the crusade brought me Joshua Delaney as well. God, *look* at him. If you can't understand me seizing him with both hands for these last few months of my life, then you're as grey on the inside as your cheap suit."

After a moment, Valeri asked, "Officer, are you actually married?" And she indicated the wedding band that Delaney wore.

"No," he replied.

Christine asked, "The affair – it's something you want? I mean … you really want it for yourself?"

Oh, this was mortifying. But it was vital that the five of them reach some kind of agreement this afternoon – otherwise Angelo was risking everything for no reason. With an effort, Delaney offered, "It's obvious what Mr. Trezini's attractions are." And indeed, he had been magnificent that afternoon. At this belated thought, Delaney sat up a little prouder.

More glances were exchanged; except for Russell who was sitting back, sullenly ignoring them all.

Valeri said, "I think we should do it."

It was shocking, the palpable change of energies in the room now that the words were spoken. Delaney looked up at Trezini, wondering if the mobster's heartbeat had sped up along with the cop's.

"Delaney," Valeri was continuing, "you need to submit your resignation from the force, effective immediately."

He hated the idea: it bore the flavor of recanting a solemn oath. "Is that really necessary?"

Reading his evident distaste, the attorney tried to soften the blow. "On paper, at least – for the sake of your cover. We need to keep you both safe."

Agent Russell bestirred himself to argue with Valeri. "Look, I'm sure Delaney appreciates Trezini's silver tongue even more than you do, but –"

While Delaney colored up yet again, Trezini chuckled and said, "Oh, believe me, he does. And the jury will love it, too."

"Come on, Russell," Valeri was saying. "Where's your courage? We wouldn't have been in these jobs so long if, deep down inside, we didn't want to try the impossible. Matthew Picano, my God …"

Eliot reminded him, "If we succeed, your career will go into orbit."

"And if we fail," Russell retorted, "can you imagine what a field day the press will have? We'll all look like idiots."

"Playing it safe hasn't gotten us anywhere with this man. Don't tell me you won't risk losing face for a cause like this."

Still prevaricating, Russell said, "I don't have the authority here and now –"

Trezini leaned forward again, and quietly asked, "Then give me your word."

A long moment stretched while they all waited on the FBI Agent. Russell looked from one to the other of them, and seemed undone by their resolve. "All right," he agreed at last. Stabbing a finger towards Delaney and Trezini, Russell said, "You're still a pair of fools, and queer fools at that. Two wild cards. But I'll do my best to get this up and running. I can't promise any more than that."

The relief and excitement brightened the room. Delaney offered Angelo a small smile, which was happily accepted.

Trezini briskly said, "You people work out the details. I need to get back to work. Josh, I'll see you tomorrow afternoon, at two?"

"Yes," Delaney replied.

"The rest of you needn't be there," Trezini continued expansively, "but Officer Delaney and I are going to give our cover a trial run. It may be the only time we'll have the whole two hours to ourselves." And this was said with the most lascivious of grins.

Delaney tried not to betray his embarrassment. The others seemed to be amused or uncomfortable, or a combination of both. Perhaps this demonstrativeness was something they would all need to grow accustomed to.

Trezini had turned away, and was heading for the door. Delaney stood, and accompanied him, figuring that a show of solidarity was the least he could offer. He murmured, "Be careful, Angelo."

Perhaps he should have expected Trezini to take advantage of the situation: the mobster was cheeky enough to press a quick kiss to Delaney's mouth before he opened the door.

There was a uniformed officer waiting outside, as requested. Trezini cheerily said to her, "Escort me off the premises!"

Desperately re-gathering an air of normality, Delaney asked, "Would you sign him out? The charges are being dropped."

He watched Trezini leave, that elegant frame tall and confident. Then Delaney closed the door, and the two cops, the Prosecuting Attorney, and the FBI Agent tried to settle down to sober business.

Delaney was at his desk, packing his few personal items into a carton. His role currently called for a display of fury and humiliation – and he didn't find it at all difficult to draw on the deep potent well of those emotions. His partner and his other colleagues were sitting there scattered throughout the squad room, watching Delaney with far more curiosity than sympathy.

At last Watson commented, "I knew you wouldn't last. You never did belong in Chicago, Delaney."

"I've done nothing wrong," Delaney angrily declared. "Nothing. It was a difficult situation, I handled it as best I could." That was obtuse enough to allow people to infer what they wanted.

Watson asked sarcastically, "So, who beat you up? Our lovely Lieutenant? Or Internal Affairs? That must have been some interview."

"Four young men with baseball bats last night, they were hardly more than children. You know, this city of yours …" Delaney had been addressing the room at large, but it soon became apparent that no one gave a damn.

So Delaney shut his mouth, flung one last indiscriminate glare around at his ex-colleagues; then he grabbed up the box, and strode out of the room.

CHAPTER FOUR

Joshua Delaney was waiting for his lover, standing at the door of room number seven at a dingy urban Comfort Inn. It was Monday of a new week, the second week of interviews already, and much to his own surprise, Delaney had found himself missing Angelo Trezini over the weekend. If the truth were to be revealed, Delaney still felt some lingering uncertainty and reluctance regarding this affair; he did, however, owe Trezini a great deal, more than Delaney could ever hope to pay. It was only fair that he give Trezini what he wanted, at least for this little while.

Agent Russell strolled out of room six and began loitering in the motel's parking lot, cigarette in hand, as if he'd been banished to smoke outside. For the sake of discretion, Delaney ignored him, which was easy enough to do; Delaney didn't even politely acknowledge him as a stranger might reasonably be expected to.

Checking his watch, Delaney saw that it was two o'clock: right on schedule Trezini drove up, parked his car in front of room seven, and walked over to Delaney. Trezini was obviously joyful at seeing his lover again – Delaney made a conscious effort to welcome him with a happy smile. It was only fair.

A couple of steps with Trezini hovering by his shoulder; and then even as the door was closing behind them Delaney and Trezini were in each other's arms, and they were kissing. Delaney still hadn't quite got the hang of this, and he was conscious of fumbling a little, while Angelo was all smooth and skillful certainty.

But then, as he'd already come to expect, Delaney's passion was provoked by this man's cleverness. Soon the two of them were each as genuine and urgent as the other. They fell across the bed, and already – still fully-dressed – Delaney found his hips were moving, and he was thrusting himself against Angelo's slim attractive frame. Any clumsiness after that was the welcome result of utter honesty.

It was barely three o'clock, and Delaney had his hand on the connecting door leading to the adjoining motel room. Trezini held the man still with a smile, and then stole one last kiss from him. Beautiful, and innocent in at least one profound kind of way: Delaney seemed completely unaware that he brought this shabby room to life. Their affair was hardly champagne, roses, and the refined comforts of the Drake hotel – but Trezini didn't need any of that. Instead, Joshua Delaney had pledged his heart and body to Trezini, despite the fact that this had come out of left field for him; and a man would be infernally greedy to want more.

Trezini was still grinning happily when he and Delaney walked through the connecting door and into room six. Russell and Valeri were waiting for them, already neck-deep in papers and files and transcripts even though they'd hardly begun to scratch the surface.

Apparently offended by Trezini's evident satisfaction, Russell complained, "I can't believe we sit around in here, while you're in there doing …" the man searched in vain for suitable words, "whatever it is that you do."

"Whatever it is that we do?" Trezini repeated mockingly. "I'm sure you can imagine enough details – or is that what bothers you?"

Russell impatiently asked, "Can we get on with this? We only have an hour."

"Funny," Trezini commented, "that's exactly what Josh said."

Valeri couldn't restrain a laugh at the humor and at Russell's evident disgust, but Trezini noted that Delaney didn't react. The police officer seemed accustomed to keeping his own counsel; and given that was showing no signs of changing, Trezini was happy enough to conclude that this was Delaney's natural demeanor rather than an unwillingness to commit himself.

Trezini sat down opposite Valeri and Russell at the motel table, which was hardly designed for such serious work: it was struggling under a clutter of recording equipment and transcripts of their previous interviews. Delaney stood in his usual place behind Trezini, ostensibly on his side but maintaining a distance.

Russell muttered, "As soon as the honeymoon's over, we'll get the full two hours."

"It'll never be over," Trezini told him.

Putting an end to extraneous conversation, Valeri pressed the record buttons and spoke in the direction of the microphone. Already this introduction was routine: "Tape four, August eleven. Interview with Mr. Carmine Trezini. Also present are Deputy Prosecuting Attorney Denise

Valeri, Special Agent Edgar Russell, and Officer Joshua Delaney." She glanced at her notes for a moment, and then looked levelly across the table. "Mr. Trezini, you ran us through a list of Picano's business interests during our last interview. Now, I've done some checking, and it all gets complicated with the number of companies and holding companies involved – but they all seem legitimate. Can you explain that?"

"Sure," Trezini replied; "you're right, they're genuine businesses. But Picano's mother lode is illegal gambling. Each of those businesses I told you about is only half the deal, each fronts for a gambling den."

Valeri was frowning in disbelief. "A laundromat?"

"They're all businesses that operate in the evenings, right? Restaurants, gas stations, laundromats … I manage one of the bars –"

"Carmine's?" she guessed.

Trezini smiled wryly at her, relieved that someone was keeping up. "Yeah, Matt named it for me. There's a door down the back where people go for poker, blackjack, roulette. The legal business provides a cover, helps launder money, gives his people legitimate employment." Trezini leaned forward, spared a glance for Russell. "You go look deeper into it. You look at who owns the properties around each of those businesses, and you look at what goes on there."

Russell wasn't impressed. "You didn't explain this before. What else are you holding out on?"

Sitting back again, Trezini dismissively said, "Give me a break. We've only just started, I'm trying to lead you through it step by step. It's not simple like his father used to do it – it's a business empire, and every part of it is half legitimate and half illegal."

"An empire?" Valeri echoed. "Surely, in the scale of things …"

"Don't let Matthew's facades fool you," Trezini said, shaking his head. "If we get far enough, we might bring the whole damned lot down with him, and then God help the city of Chicago."

Apparently Valeri didn't know whether to be impressed or not. Leaving that decision aside for now, she prompted, "What's the next step, Mr. Trezini?"

"He's wanting to take over the fight business, boxing. It's a new interest for him, so maybe that makes him vulnerable for a while. This might be your chance to watch how he does it, how he sets it all up."

"It will be half legitimate again?" Valeri asked.

"Yeah. On one hand he's looking at a string of gyms, contracts on fighters, promotion of matches, what have you. The other side of it is large scale betting, fixing fights, that kind of thing. Do you see how it works?" Trezini decided to give them another example. "He has a legitimate security firm, and it does good business – but they also do the heavy stuff for him, the shady stuff. They collect protection money, solve problems, keep everyone in their place."

Russell said, "And what about you?"

Trezini nodded. "It's the same for everyone who works for him – I manage the bar but I also manage the gambling den behind it. Everyone has twice the stake in maintaining the status quo, and everyone knows just enough to take Matthew very seriously indeed, though no one sees all of it – maybe not even Matthew himself, by now!"

But Valeri wanted to backtrack. "If you're not part of the security firm, then what were you doing at Smith's warehouse the other night? You told Delaney that was about protection money."

"Sure. I'm not his right-hand man – he doesn't have one – but Picano trusts me. I'm in the inner circle. And I have a little more style than his regular thugs, I have a larger vocabulary. So, he uses me for collections and negotiations that require a little finesse."

"Finesse," Russell flatly repeated, apparently skeptical.

Trezini grinned at them. "Oh yeah."

The bar now known as Carmine's had been doing such poor business that Picano had bought it for a bargain basement price. He'd turned it over to Trezini to run, secure in the knowledge that the gambling den he installed behind it would bring in enough customers and money to cover any ongoing losses. Trezini had, however, discovered a knack for this kind of work and he'd taken pride in turning the bar's fortunes around.

While the place was small in size, a stylish refit had helped develop a quietly convivial atmosphere. People enjoyed relaxing here amidst the subtle lighting and comfortable booths, with no clocks in sight. Trezini found that he enjoyed playing the gracious host, and ensuring that his staff provided good service when it was wanted and discretion when it wasn't.

Even Matthew Picano himself had developed the habit of visiting Trezini here, on at least one evening or maybe two a week. Tonight, he was sitting in his usual place at the end of the bar furthest from the front door, and Trezini was pouring them each a generous nip of brandy. The two men were comfortable with each other; though Trezini noted that all the bartenders, and those of the customers who recognized Picano, maintained a wary and discreet distance. As well they might.

When Trezini brought the drinks over and sat next to this most familiar of acquaintances, Picano picked up their interrupted conversation. "Do you know what Smith is doing? Ordering truckloads of food and produce, legitimately – then having his goons hijack the trucks. He claims the insurance, he's got the goods anyway, he cleans up big. And he's too greedy to share."

Grimacing, Trezini observed, "The guy's been learning from you. He never used to be that smart."

"Oh, he's getting smarter in some ways, but he's still real dumb in others. Trying to buck me out of my cut," Picano grumbled, "not wanting to pay for my protection –" he amended that with a wry smile – "for my security consultancy. That's just plain dumb."

"You're right about that."

Picano said, deadly serious, "He's going to need a lesson taught, sooner rather than later."

"You've tried talking to him?" When Picano nodded, Trezini asked, "He's unrepentant?"

"I told him, you put one of my people, you put my childhood friend in a freezer, and you throw a cop in there after him – you need to learn about respect."

"Respect? How about some simple common sense."

"We've got a lid on the situation," Picano continued, "that's fine. I don't like how the police are putting a lid on it, too, though – something's going on there, something crooked, we need to figure that out. But as for Smith, I've cut him more than enough slack. If he doesn't make the payment he promised me next month, he's losing a son. And, Cat: *you* can have the honor."

Trezini just said easily, "Thanks, Matt."

"Yeah, I thought that'd make you feel better." Picano was looking smug, no doubt liking the tidiness and thoroughness of his solution. "This time I'll make sure you've got back-up, I'm not having anything else go wrong. But that's for after you collect a penalty payment on O'Donnell's loan, all right?"

One of the bartenders had been hovering at a careful distance – once he caught Trezini's eye, he came closer. "Customers, sir."

Nodding in acknowledgement, Trezini looked around to see an older well-off couple waiting, sipping drinks at the bar. They were long-standing regulars and therefore due the discreet red-carpet treatment. Trezini walked over to welcome them, murmuring, "How are you doing tonight? It's good to see you again."

He escorted the couple past Picano – neither the couple nor Picano deigned to recognize each other – and around a corner to a door hidden from general view behind the bar. Once he'd unlocked the door, Trezini ushered them in. "Best of luck to you, sir, ma'am."

Taking a moment, Trezini glanced around at the card tables, surrounded by people and piled in cash. Everything seemed to be humming along smoothly, so he closed the door firmly, ensuring that it locked, and rejoined Picano.

The two men sat in silence for a time, sipping at the fine brandy. "So," Trezini eventually observed, "other than a few minor problems, it sounds as if business is good."

Picano smiled happily, smug once more. "There are benefits to being king of the castle, Cat, and one is that I get everything to go my way."

Trezini couldn't help returning the grin. "Sounds like you're having fun, too."

"Oh yeah – why else would I do it?" Picano considered Trezini for a moment. "And you're still out there having your own kind of fun, huh?"

"Oh yeah," Trezini echoed, his grin broadening. "I'm in love."

Picano shook his head, bemused. "Whatever," he said.

"Well, you can at least see that he's gorgeous, can't you?" Trezini pushed, tongue-in-cheek. "Absolutely gorgeous. I figured that much wasn't in question."

"I don't know, Cat. I just don't know."

And Trezini decided to change the topic again. It would be worse than foolish to dwell on such matters in Picano's company – because if Matthew glimpsed anything of what Angelo and Josh were doing in conjunction with their affair, then Trezini wouldn't live to see any of it through.

Delaney lay on his unwelcoming bed in the sanctuary of his apartment, masturbating. Over recent years he'd rarely had even this much of a sex life; he now felt as if he were waking from a long sleep. And the sleep hadn't been a bad thing, not in itself, but Angelo Trezini had woken him from it, and Delaney suspected that nothing in his life would ever be quite the same again.

Already there was a significant change – already the generic blue-tinted monochrome movie in his mind was being overlaid with another image, replaced with something more colorful. Instead of anonymous or long-ago or faraway women, there was a lean masculine body, and green-hazel eyes glowing with fervor, and a mouth that knew how to do exquisite things. A presumptuous man, with many admirable qualities, who needed Delaney … who regularly declared that he loved Delaney. Who whispered *Josh* in fond tones at moments such as this …

Delaney came, a soft moan echoing around the empty room.

The sound recalled him to himself, and he lay there silent and still again. Considering.

Trezini was right: Delaney was fascinated by the man who was so many things that Delaney was not. Trezini was a book full and overflowing with words, a book Delaney wanted to read all the way through – while Delaney felt as if he himself was a blank slate who was only now being written upon.

He enjoyed Trezini's company, there was no denying it. And he certainly enjoyed – Well. Delaney had never before seriously imagined having sex with a man, but the sex was good, surprisingly good. Damned good, if the truth were told. And Delaney was sure that wasn't only due to the long sleep, the period of abstinence that hadn't quite been by choice. Perhaps the passion of it would fade over time, but for now Delaney was happy enough with the arrangement.

And he felt so horribly guilty at getting Trezini into this. Delaney shifted over onto his side, and curled up around the hurt of his thoughtlessness. Trezini had been vulnerable and Delaney had unwittingly taken advantage – and Delaney would have done a lot more than have sex with the man to try making it up to him. A lot more. He wondered if Trezini knew that.

Eventually Delaney forced himself back to soothing images, memories of how it had been to fall asleep with his arms around his lover. *Goodnight, Josh,* Angelo whispered for him, and that was the last thing Delaney heard that night.

Lofty stone arches lifted over him as Trezini knelt in the front pew, praying.

The comfort and mystery of his church's shadows were only enhanced by the dim light filtering through a stained glass window high above. This time Trezini wasn't alone: the priest was kneeling next to him, and they were praying together, lips moving silently. *For Thine is the kingdom, the power and the glory, for ever and ever. Amen.*

Once they were done, they both sat back; and, consciously or not, they contemplated the altar.

If Trezini had ever before experienced this sense of peace, this core of well-being, he had long forgotten it. "Father," he murmured, "I feel truly forgiven. For the first time since I was eighteen, I actually feel that God has forgiven me."

The priest was regarding him with grace and understanding; but he was too wise a man, having lived in this neighborhood for decades, to ask Trezini any questions.

Having caught up with O'Donnell in one of Picano's nightclubs, Trezini escorted him out through the back into a suitably dark and grimy alley. O'Donnell was already cowering, being smart enough to recognize trouble when he was deep in it; he was propped back against the nearest brick wall as if he needed it in order to remain upright. Trezini stood there facing him, maintaining a relaxed but businesslike manner. One of Picano's goons loomed at Trezini's shoulder, as promised, though Trezini really didn't need the back-up. The club's music was muted out here, but it was loud enough to help mask this conversation and its inevitable outcome.

"But four percent per week!" O'Donnell was protesting. "It's impossible! If Mr. Picano would consider even *three* percent, I'd be able to pay him regular as clockwork."

Trezini said evenly, "I was very clear with you about the terms of the loan, O'Donnell."

"You were, Mr. Trezini, very clear indeed. But I was so desperate I didn't think it through. Can't we renegotiate? I'm sure we can work something out, I'd be happy to meet you more than halfway."

"Mr. Picano might reconsider the terms. But that doesn't affect the penalty payment – that's due now."

O'Donnell continued to grovel. "Please, I know I shouldn't have missed the payments. But can't you talk to him? I know he trusts you, Mr. Trezini.

I know Mr. Picano listens to you."

"Yes, he does," Trezini agreed. "He listens to me because I'm a man of my word. Did you think I was just fooling around?"

"No –" And it seemed that O'Donnell was belatedly recalling one of the terms of his loan. It was obvious even in the darkness of the alley that his face paled and his eyes blanked in fear.

Trezini smoothly continued, "Then be a man of your word, O'Donnell, and let me take the penalty payment. I'll discuss the terms for the balance of the loan with Mr. Picano, but that's his decision." And Trezini pulled an appropriately mean-looking switchblade from his pocket, flicked it open.

The goon was useful in holding O'Donnell in place against the wall while Trezini efficiently went to work. O'Donnell let loose with one sharp scream but it was lost against the muted music. When he was done, Trezini bound the wound to prevent an excessive loss of blood, and then sent the goon to alert the club's bouncers. O'Donnell didn't have to die, after all.

Denise Valeri wasn't spending much time in her office these days. All those years of clambering the rungs as a Deputy Prosecuting Attorney – and when she finally got to the point of having her own office, she was spending most of her days here in the federal building with the FBI or in a cheap motel room with Agent Edgar Russell. Well, Valeri supposed it was a small price to pay for the sake of such direct involvement in this case. "Matthew Picano, my God," she murmured once more to herself. Who'd have thought it?

Well, somehow Carmine Trezini and Joshua Delaney had dreamed up the inconceivable and, luckily for Denise Valeri, she'd been invited along for the ride. Between them, they'd awoken ideals and impulses Valeri thought she'd had knocked out of her in college.

If anyone else was feeling lucky about working on this case, it wasn't in evidence. The team members assembled by the FBI were strewn throughout an open-plan office – and every last one of them appeared tired and confused and frustrated.

Well, perhaps that was inevitable. Thoroughly working through all of Trezini's information on Picano was going to involve more time and effort than anyone could reasonably provide. Even this early into the investigation, the room was full of paper and files, what with transcripts of Trezini's interviews, associated company and financial records, criminal records, and who knew what else. So much paperwork involved …

… and of all these people, only Valeri and Russell had any direct contact with the unexpectedly quixotic and rather charming Carmine Angelo Trezini. What occasionally troubled Valeri was that even Russell didn't really seem to care about the man who was making all this possible. Not that Valeri had unrealistic or unnecessary notions of them all being buddies – Trezini would be a difficult person to get to know, after all – but it didn't seem *safe* for these people to consider Trezini as nothing more than a name and a file number.

Valeri was still absently mulling this over late that night, as she sat up in bed re-reading one of the transcripts. Perhaps it wouldn't create a problem. Well, perhaps it was simply an insoluble problem because the more people who had contact with Trezini, the greater the danger he'd be in. Valeri sighed, and rummaged through the other paperwork scattered across the bed, looking for a file reference to jot down against one of the mobster's responses. None of this was easy.

Jeffrey, the man Denise had been living with for almost six years now, wandered into the bedroom carrying two mugs of tea. Valeri looked up at him with a grateful smile, though she knew she must appear somewhat distracted.

Returning the smile, Jeffrey seemed to come to a decision. He put the mugs down on the bedside table – then abruptly swept most of the paperwork off the bed with an extravagant gesture, and launched himself onto his significant other, passionate and considerate all at once.

Valeri really had to admire the man. She laughed, and succumbed.

CHAPTER FIVE

"God help the city of Chicago," Valeri intoned, recalling Trezini's words. Valeri, Russell and Delaney were loitering in room six at the Comfort Inn, waiting on the mobster. Three weeks of interviews had produced an unwieldy mess of files and transcripts. Looking around her, Valeri continued, "It's too much, this is too big. I had no idea Picano owns half of Chicago. He must be worth millions. Yet he behaves like he's small fry."

"I suspect it's partly protective camouflage," Delaney offered.

"Camouflage, so that – so that we know what he is, but we don't take him quite seriously enough?"

Delaney nodded. "I believe there's also a deeper reason, though. These people have a very real love for their neighborhood, their homes, their families. Maybe Picano has no wish to live any other way."

Russell said, "Maybe he just can't conceive of living any other way. Me, I would have retired in luxury by now." Ever the cynic …

"No, you wouldn't," Valeri retorted. "What you choose to do with your life, and what Picano chooses to do with his – these aren't occupations you can just walk away from."

"Talk to Delaney here. He's the one on a crusade, not me."

Valeri settled for grimacing at the man and changing the topic. "Look, can you get more of your people investigating? We're not keeping up with Trezini."

Russell shrugged. "Does it matter? The case won't be going to court for months yet, if not years."

"Of course it matters! We need to stay on top of this, for Trezini's sake if no one else's." Valeri left a pause, but Delaney didn't leap in to second the motion. The three of them avoided each other's gazes for a long moment. Eventually Valeri disconsolately added, "My God, I'm glad it's only three hours a week."

The clock measured time with loud ticks. It was almost two already. Delaney excused himself with a polite nod, and headed out through the connecting door, leaving Russell and Valeri to their own devices.

Joshua Delaney stood waiting for Trezini at the door of room seven. When the man arrived, Delaney greeted him with a small but genuine smile. This was getting easier all the time and Trezini was invariably more than happy to see him, which was too flattering an attitude not to have an impact.

Today Trezini walked up to Delaney, reaching out a hand that Delaney instinctively held in his – and Trezini murmured, "I've been followed. Kiss me."

Even as he chastised himself for the slip, Delaney's smile lost its edge. If Trezini was feeling any dismay he was hiding it far more effectively. But perhaps it didn't matter because within the space of a breath, Trezini was in Delaney's arms, and they were kissing … Trying to gather his wits, Delaney stepped backwards, drawing Trezini inside with him even as their embrace deepened – and then Delaney reached out with one arm and swung the door firmly closed, shutting out the world as best he could.

There was vague embarrassment at the thought of having been witnessed kissing a man but anxiety was the stronger of Delaney's reactions. Trezini had disengaged himself and walked over to peer out through the net curtains. Finding himself stupidly hovering on the spot, Delaney asked, "Does this mean that Picano suspects?"

"No," Trezini replied easily enough. "No, the guy's gone already. No doubt feeling absolutely disgusted with what he just saw. If it's obvious we're having an affair, Matthew won't bother looking any further. He's checking up on us, that's all." At last Trezini turned around – and then he paused, apparently in order to drink in the sight of Delaney. "God, I don't see you enough," the man declared, heartfelt. "I don't see enough of you. Only three hours a week."

"Anything more and we risk our cover," Delaney reminded him. But then he admitted, "I don't like knowing that you're out there, and I can't protect you."

Trezini smiled, though he seemed sad. "There's no need to worry so much, Josh."

Not caring to argue about such a matter, Delaney just held out his hands. Trezini promptly strode over to him, and they embraced again. Delaney was already beginning to suspect that his arms provided a place in which Trezini felt he belonged. There were other places for Trezini, though; other people he belonged with, just as significant to him if not more so.

"We have maybe a few months," Trezini was murmuring. "A few months in which to meet, fall in love, have sex, marry, argue, reconcile, have more sex, argue some more, completely exhaust each other sexually, grow old and grey together." He was nuzzling against Delaney's throat, sounding content despite envisaging a rather short-term future for the relationship. "A few months. But some people don't do even half those things in a lifetime."

Delaney quietly declared, "We'll have longer than that if I have anything to do with it."

Trezini didn't seem reassured. They kissed, but the sadness remained.

"Do you know what seems odd to me?" Delaney asked, wanting to build on the connection between them. "I know the most fundamental things about you, Angelo – but the day-to-day things, I hardly know at all." And he promised, "We'll have our chance for that, though."

That earned him a reluctant grin. "Yeah. Sometime or other, we'll get to sleep every night in each other's arms."

"We'll have the chance to not mind about sharing a toothbrush," Delaney added.

"We'll argue over who gets the first shower and all the hot water, and who gets to lie in bed another ten minutes." Trezini's spirits seemed to have been restored.

Delaney smiled. "Oh, that's easy to resolve. We'll both lie in bed an extra ten minutes, and then we'll shower together."

Trezini was gazing at him with the most bewitching glow in his eyes. No one had ever needed Joshua Delaney even half as much as this man did. After a moment, the two of them began kissing again, kissing with happy hunger, and Delaney gathered Angelo close before falling with him onto the bed.

In room six, Valeri was occupying herself with the ever-increasing paperwork. She had become quite practiced at ignoring Russell, who was sitting there wearing headphones, listening with a preoccupied scowl on his face.

Eventually, the FBI Agent tore the headphones off and announced, "Someone followed Trezini here, one of Picano's people." At Valeri's look of concern, Russell shrugged. "Trezini thinks it's nothing to worry about."

Valeri nodded her acceptance of this, knowing that she could trust Trezini's survival instincts. Instead, she asked testily, "Is it really necessary to listen in?"

Russell grimaced. "Not now! They're at it again, they won't surface until three."

That almost won a smirk out of Valeri. "You sound … resentful."

"*I* should get lucky this often," Russell grumbled. Then he said, "You know, I bet Trezini won't bother telling us he was followed. He's playing his own game, he's arranging this exactly the way he wants it. I don't reckon even Delaney knows half of what's going on."

"Well, do you blame him? I'd think Trezini is entitled to do this his way, given the risk he's taking. And you can't deny he's giving us good information."

"Yeah…" But the agreement sounded so unwilling.

Valeri fixed the man with a stare. "He's giving us damned good information through the interviews. Have you learned *anything* of use by eavesdropping on them?"

A shrug, and Russell mumbled, "Standard operating procedure."

"Yeah, wonderful."

Russell grimaced again, and gave in. "Okay, okay," he said. "Give me that last transcript to read again."

And Valeri handed some of the paperwork over.

Trezini and his mother were washing up together after their early evening meal. They had been a family of two for years now, and they worked comfortably together out of habit and out of a desire that it be exactly so between them. Rinsing off the last of the saucepans, Trezini handed it to his mother to dry, and then cleaned the sink while letting the water drain away.

When the two of them didn't have company, Trezini had gotten his mother away from the old-fashioned old-country notion that she shouldn't sit or eat in the presence of men. He brewed a pot of coffee while she put away the plates and cutlery, and then they sat together at the kitchen table for a while, mugs steaming before them.

Neither of them talked much these days. There was a mutual avoidance of anything to do with Matthew Picano and Trezini's crusade against him, on the basis that they agreed to disagree about the necessity of it all. And Angelo had soon discovered that his mother didn't want to know anything about Joshua Delaney, either. So they sat there in silence, enjoying each other's company, and holding hands. Eventually, though, Trezini kissed his mother goodbye before heading to Carmine's for an evening's work.

There was something very bittersweet about the mood this family currently shared, Trezini reflected, which was perhaps only to be expected; for both mother and son assumed that Angelo must soon be killed.

Delaney had received reluctant agreement from Lieutenant Eliot and Agent Russell for him to join the FBI's task force investigating Matthew Picano. This was, of course, on the strict understanding that he be careful not to destroy his cover as a married freelance writer. Delaney felt he probably would have agreed to any condition: he needed something to help him fill his days; he needed to feel that he was still a police officer, even though he wore plain clothes; and he needed to do anything he could in order to help Angelo Trezini.

It was soon apparent that the Bureau's local resources were being stretched to breaking point by the case, and yet Delaney never quite felt that his assistance was welcomed. Perhaps any outsider was mistrusted. Or perhaps ... well, perhaps no one here knew how to handle the fact that this cop – this ex-cop – was conducting a homosexual affair with the case's main witness.

Even after these weeks together, Delaney wasn't entirely sure what to make of that fact himself. But there was no denying his life had taken this turn, and no arguing with what he felt when Trezini was in his arms, when Angelo was kissing him. When the mobster gazed at Delaney with those green-hazel eyes; fascinated and fascinating, trusted and trusting. When they were both naked, moving in their already-familiar body-to-body caress, finding the most profound pleasure together in the most simple of acts ...

This was really not the time or the place to indulge in sexual fantasies. After all, the FBI was hardly an environment that welcomed or even condoned such interactions between men.

Seeking distraction and discipline, Delaney walked over to a whiteboard and studied the chart on it. He had provided the final link in it himself, the previous day: the chart demonstrated the ownership links between Picano and Carmine's bar, and those between Picano and the gambling den behind the bar. There were several companies and holding companies and individuals involved, and the two chains of ownership were quite separate, so it had been a difficult process to prove the links conclusively.

It was only now that Delaney was beginning to appreciate why the FBI used to insist all its agents hold a degree in accounting: such knowledge was vital in understanding the financial side of the kind of crimes they investigated. Delaney had to admit that he had trouble keeping up sometimes, as his formal education had never progressed beyond high school. Trying to make up for the lack, he was reading accounting texts and financial newspapers during the long evenings he spent alone in his apartment.

Delaney shuffled through the table of evidentiary paperwork that was summarized by the whiteboard charts: the company records and the property deeds, the annual reports and other legal documents. Two of the companies, he noted, were named Sky Hook Holdings and Blue Skies, which perhaps betrayed a touch of whimsy on someone's part. Delaney wondered whether that was Picano – and he thought that if so then it was a trait that Trezini no doubt would have enjoyed.

Picano and Trezini had been friends, had shared their lives growing up in this neighborhood. And then Delaney had met Trezini, and naively promised the mobster redemption, and the friends would become mortal enemies as a result. *This crusade is something I have to do,* Delaney remembered Trezini declaring. *And I'll be dead by the end of it, if not sooner.* Delaney repressed a shudder. He needed to do anything he could for Trezini. He needed to ensure that the mobster – the ex-mobster – didn't pay that price.

There was a folder of maps and plans here amid the files, showing those of Picano's legitimate businesses that had gambling dens linked to them. Delaney flipped through the folder, and took a moment to gaze at the floor-plan for Carmine's bar. Trezini worked there, and it was of course too dangerous for Delaney to ever visit. Imagination would have to suffice.

Finally finding the plans relating to the gambling den behind Cin Cin, the restaurant where Delaney had been introduced to Picano, the cop headed back to his desk. It was time to start work on proving another chain of ownership links.

CHAPTER SIX

Trezini sat slumped in his chair in Picano's office, head resting against the high wooden back despite the carving making uncomfortable dents in his skull. He'd been leading a busy life already, running the bar and the gambling den, and coping with the myriad details of being a member of Picano's inner circle, and there'd always been his mother to take good care of. On top of that, Trezini was now conducting an intense love affair and dealing with the FBI. The demanding pace was going to kill him if Matthew didn't get in there first.

Having just dozed through one of the inner circle's regular meetings, Trezini was now spending his usual few moments alone with his old buddy Picano, entertaining vague thoughts of finding enough energy to ask Nicola for a strong coffee. It was just as well Picano was in a chatty mood and prepared to fill in the silences.

"One of the boxers I'm managing now," Matthew was saying, "is Nathan Walsh – maybe you've heard of him?"

Trezini stirred himself to shake his head in the negative, unable to get as excited by the fight business as Picano obviously was.

"Well …" Matthew said, dragging out the word in order to gain Trezini's attention, "Nathan Walsh is gay."

"Ah," said Trezini, really not giving a damn.

"He was surprised I figured it out so quickly," Picano said, patently pleased with himself. "I told him he was doing me good, he's boosting my equal opportunity employment quotas. Who says I'm not full of community spirit?"

Trezini obediently shared a laugh at this hoary joke of Picano's, despite the fact it had worn rather thin on him over the years.

Picano continued in thoughtful tones, "You know, I figure Nathan fights so well because he's had to, being gay. He's had to prove himself, defend himself."

"Maybe," Trezini offered, preventing himself from rolling his eyes at this naive theory. He'd bet good money that Matthew had actually said to the guy, *One of my best friends is gay.*

The thing about having grown up with Matthew Picano was that Trezini remembered all the silly brash moments, all the petty humiliations of being a teenager, all the stupidities, all the times Picano had lost or been thwarted. That meant Trezini could see past the handsome charismatic powerful surface to the child cowering not too far below. In fact, it was a wonder Matt kept him around, for his buddy Cat knew the mob boss was only human after all. Then again, Picano had probably assumed all along that he had Trezini wrapped round his little finger, which wasn't too far from the truth.

But now, in the name of his own redemption, Trezini was going to destroy the man.

The truth remained that this crusade wasn't about Matthew; it was about Angelo. Matthew himself was almost irrelevant. Nevertheless, he would be a casualty, as would Nicola and their children. Nothing would ever be the same for any of them.

Trezini slowly became aware that the gaze he'd turned to his companion had softened.

Picano was watching him with an odd puzzled little smile. Finally the man said, "Walsh is a decent kind of guy. And he's handsome, I guess. Maybe I should get the two of you together."

"You're matchmaking for me?" Trezini asked, almost surprised and amused enough to laugh. "Thanks, Matt, but I found my true love already."

"A married guy?" Serious, confidential tones from Matthew now. "He'll never leave his wife for you, Cat, trust me on that. Where's the future in it?"

"There *is* no future in it. There's just the here and now. And that's wonderful."

Picano shook his head, smiling ruefully for a moment. "Yeah, you're still glowing and it's been, what? Five weeks? But he's using you, Cat. Where does he live? Some nice suburban place with a lawn and a picket fence? Does he have kids? A golden Labrador? How does he feel about his beautiful wife?"

Trezini pushed himself up in his chair, more than a little annoyed by this latest interrogation. "What's with the questions, Matt? Have you been trying to check him out?"

"You're going to get hurt –"

"Yes, I am," Trezini snapped.

"– when he realizes there are better looking guys than you out there, who are just as easy."

Taking a sharp breath, Trezini stared at the man. It seemed that Matthew was trying to hurt him and warn him all at once. How about that? Well, Trezini was indeed going to be hurt, though not in the way that Picano anticipated. Trezini decided to offer something for Matt to think about after Angelo's redemption; a morsel of comfort for his old friend, and a last brazen message for his new enemy.

"It'll be worth it, Matt. Remember I said that, okay?"

Picano met his stare for a long moment. And then at last he gave up, shrugging as if Trezini was really none of his concern. "You'll get hurt, it'll be worth it," he repeated in easy tones. He was already turning his attention to the paperwork on his desk. "Sure, Cat."

Delaney was waiting yet again for his lover at the Comfort Inn, reflecting with some surprise on how content he felt. He hadn't realized how unsure his life had become until now, with this rediscovery of certainty. When Trezini drove up, just before two o'clock, the welcoming smile Delaney summoned was effortlessly genuine.

In unexpected contrast, Trezini seemed rather dispirited. The two of them headed inside without speaking.

As soon as the door had closed out the rest of the world, Delaney drew Trezini into his arms, and leaned back against the wall to hold the man's weight against him. His embrace deliberately echoed how the cop had held the mobster for warmth in the freezer when they'd first met.

Long moments eased by. And then Trezini murmured, "If I had a crush on Matthew until I hit twenty, that's not a part of this. If he used my feelings against me, that's not a part of this. If wanting him was kind of why I decided to work for him, that's really not a part of this at all."

Delaney had turned his head a little, so that his mouth pressed a kiss to Angelo's close-cropped head.

"It was *my* decision," Trezini continued in firmer tones, "and this is *my* redemption. It's not about revenge. It's about making the right decision, after all these years."

"I know," Delaney offered.

"I love you, Josh."

Delaney's lips curved in a happy smile that Angelo would feel rather than see. "I know that, too."

Trezini let out a sigh.

Gently disengaging from the embrace for a moment, Delaney led Trezini over to the bed. They lay down together on top of the covers, and then Delaney simply held the man close, still fully-clothed. He didn't know what else to do for him.

Valeri and Russell were waiting. Russell kept casting glances between the clock and the connecting door, becoming steadily more anxious because Trezini and Delaney had always been scrupulously punctual until now. Finally, at ten past three, Russell grabbed up the headphones and listened with a furious frown.

"Nothing!" he tersely told Valeri, letting the equipment fall to the table. "I knew it – they've skipped out on us!" And he rushed over to fling open the connecting door.

Concerned for the two men, Valeri followed Russell. When the FBI Agent stumbled to an abrupt halt just inside the next room, Valeri peered over his shoulder – and she saw Delaney and Trezini lying there together on the bed.

Of course they hadn't run. Perhaps they should, though, Valeri found herself thinking. At the intrusion, Trezini had buried his face further into the other man's shoulder. As for Delaney, he appeared so achingly compassionate that he almost broke Valeri's heart. He was holding Trezini close in an embrace that was raw, tender, comforting … It was an infinitely more intimate moment than if she and Russell had broken in on them naked and having sex.

The stillness held for a dazed moment, and then Delaney glanced up at the clock in their room. It seemed he was surprised by the time. "I'm sorry," Delaney muttered, his voice thick with dazed emotion. "Can you give us another minute or two?"

Russell was of course feeling nothing but embarrassment by now. "Yeah. Sorry."

Ever-so-quietly, he and Valeri withdrew into the other room, easing the door closed behind them. Valeri sat down to patiently wait, trusting that Delaney would ensure Trezini took whatever time he needed.

Russell wouldn't settle, though: he paced to and fro, movements unusually uncoordinated. Eventually he said in fierce tones, "Something's happened! What do you figure?"

"I don't know," Valeri softly replied.

"You watch: they're going to skip out on us if we're not careful." Russell sounded portentous.

To which Valeri's only thought was that she wouldn't blame them if they did. So she remained silent.

Delaney shifted the barest fraction to once more bestow a kiss on Angelo's shorn head. The two of them had hardly moved at all during the hour they'd spent together: Delaney's body felt unwieldy as a result. "Angelo?" he whispered. "Do you want to call off today's interview?"

The man sighed. But soon he said, "No. No, let's do it." And he began the slow process of extricating himself from his lover's embrace. Delaney found himself surprisingly reluctant to let Trezini go.

Soon they had gathered themselves enough to walk into the next room, fifteen minutes late. Valeri was at the table in her usual place but instead of sitting beside her, Russell was hovering at a distance; restless, unhappy. Trezini sat down opposite Valeri, perfectly composed. If the man was feeling any reluctance, he didn't betray it. However, no one seemed prepared to meet anyone else's gaze.

Deciding that Trezini deserved a demonstration of support, Delaney brought a chair over and sat close to him – Trezini glanced at him in surprise for a moment, before smiling in gentle gratification for the gesture.

At last Valeri broke the silence and began the interview. "Tape fifteen, September eighth. Interview with Mr. Carmine Trezini, in the presence of Valeri, Russell and Delaney."

Russell paced closer and demanded, "What's happened? What's going on?"

Silence resounded for a moment. Then Trezini said, "Nothing. Nothing's happened."

"Then what the hell was *that* about?"

A hard challenge fell through Trezini's face and voice. "Don't you know? Weren't you listening in?"

Russell became defensively furious. "No," he abruptly said.

Valeri weakly backed the FBI Agent up. "He wasn't listening. We weren't …"

Another long pause. Delaney felt absolutely mortified at the thought of himself and Trezini being overheard; their conversations, their private declarations, their love-making. Perhaps he should have expected as much – Angelo obviously did. Eventually Delaney managed to offer a diplomatic explanation: "You should understand this isn't the easiest thing for Mr. Trezini to do."

"Of course," Valeri murmured.

Delaney was already continuing, "He's known Mr. Picano all his life." Though maybe even that was saying too much. He resisted the urge to apologize to Angelo.

"I imagine we're all prey to occasional doubts; Mr. Trezini most of all." Valeri glanced over her shoulder at Russell, and then looked across at the cop and the mobster. "All right," she said, "shall we move along?" When no one protested, she checked her notes and began. "Mr. Trezini, the body found in Lake Michigan yesterday – do you know anything about it?"

"Oh yeah," Trezini said easily. "Smith – the guy who inadvertently started all this because he threw Delaney into his freezer with me? Smith has forgotten that Picano is king of the castle around here. Picano's waiting on a payment. He suggested I whack one of Smith's sons if the guy defaults."

Valeri frowned over this. "We haven't identified the corpse yet, but surely Smith would have claimed the body if it was his son."

"It isn't his son," announced Trezini.

"What – Picano backed down?"

Trezini shook his head. "Matthew isn't stupid enough to threaten something he won't follow through on. No, the body was one of Smith's thugs – he brought a message to Picano that wasn't well received. Picano had Genari do it, as a reply."

"You know that for sure?" Valeri asked.

"Hey, I was there. The slugs are from a nine millimeter, right? Two shots, one in the heart, one in the back of the head. If you ask me, Picano was overreacting – but his father would have done something like it weeks before."

Valeri seemed a little taken aback. "Well, okay, so you know that for sure. What else has he followed through on?" She thought for a moment, no doubt keen to progress some outstanding cases. "There was a messy business a few weeks ago – some idiot had his thumb cut off. At first he was babbling about a penalty in a loan-sharking deal, but then he shut up."

Trezini let out a cynical laugh. "He actually went to a legitimate hospital? What a moron."

"You know about that?" Valeri asked. "I think his name was Connolly. O'Connell."

"O'Donnell. Yeah, I know about that," Trezini announced: "because I did it."

The three law enforcement people exchanged looks. It seemed that none of them quite knew what to do with this news. Even Delaney felt startled, though he supposed he shouldn't have been. Had they all forgotten for a while just who they were dealing with?

Trezini was continuing with a rather disconcerting breeziness. "What can I say? He knew the penalty for missing payments, and Picano wasn't about to let the matter slide."

With massive sarcasm, Russell commented, "Oh yeah, that's right – he uses you for negotiations that require finesse."

Trezini looked from Russell to Valeri, finding only distaste. That wasn't so unexpected, surely. Amputating someone's thumb, presumably without the benefit of anesthetic, was a terrible penalty in itself. But of course it wasn't only the immediate effects – the man would be crippled for the rest of his life.

With trepidation obvious to anyone who knew him, Trezini now turned to his lover. And Delaney didn't hide the fact that he was troubled by what Trezini had done. However, he said, "We all knew Mr. Trezini's background. I, for one, respect his honesty. Perhaps you should continue the interview, Ms. Valeri."

A moment passed. Valeri was sitting back stiffly in her chair while Russell looked as sour as lemons. They were obviously still feeling rather challenged by the situation.

Trezini offered, "Do you want to know who whacked old Carbonne last year?"

Valeri blurted out, "It wasn't you?"

"No."

"Well, then, yes," Valeri said. "Of course. Any help with any unsolved cases would be –"

"It was Victor Murray," Trezini said, interrupting her. "Strangled him with his bare hands. You'll find Vic in Detroit under an old alias."

"All right."

Trezini sketched a grin. "This is too easy. What about the bank job last October?"

Valeri nodded with some encouragement, having started to regain her equilibrium.

"Oh, and before I forget – I don't know what went down Thursday last week, but two of Matt's goons came to Carmine's; there were spots of blood all down their shirts and pants. These guys were wanting my help – it's always, 'Trez, what do I do now? Trez, I'm stuck, help me out here.' But, for God's sake, I told them I have a dress code in the bar, you know. And they just said, 'Hell, Trez, we're wearing suits and ties!'" Trezini laughed at his tale, and seemed heartened by Delaney's offered smile.

"Give me their names," Valeri was saying, "and I'll see if anything's on the books. Then tell me about the bank job."

For the first time, the interview continued past four o'clock.

Delaney accompanied Trezini out through the connecting door and into their room, heading for the external door. Despite the interview having eventually turned out well and despite the range of new information being appreciated, Trezini was looking worried again. Just as Delaney put his hand on the door handle, Trezini muttered, "That thing with O'Donnell's damned thumb …"

"You know," Delaney said easily, "I think that Ms. Valeri and Mr. Russell have ended up rather liking you, Angelo. And you shocked them."

Trezini drew closer, so that they were talking with no more than a few inches between them, though they weren't touching. "I don't care about them – what about you?"

Delaney closed his eyes for a moment, and then looked very directly at his lover. "If you and I didn't both have a streak of ruthlessness, we wouldn't be working against Picano. I understand. You were doing your job."

"That's enough for you?" The words sounded so raw, so rough.

"It has to be. Angelo, there are things I've done through my job that I'm not proud of."

"You never cut off anyone's thumb, though."

"No," Delaney agreed, and again he didn't hide his dismay over this thing that Trezini had done, for Angelo deserved his honesty.

Trezini stared at him for a long moment, and then with a sigh the man tilted his head forward so that they were resting brow against brow. Delaney drew him into a hug, endeavoring to convey reassurance, though he couldn't deny that the mood between them remained difficult.

Eventually, Trezini drew away and walked out through the door with a regretful look but without their customary farewell kiss. Delaney stood there watching him go. Even after Trezini's car had disappeared into the traffic, the cop didn't turn away and head back to the other room.

Two days later, Trezini still hadn't shaken a creeping sense of unease. He couldn't afford to alienate the only person in the world he could truly count as a friend. Although Trezini wasn't really questioning Delaney's personal loyalty, the mobster was more worried about his own miscalculation. He'd thought a no-bones-about-it confession would be the most acceptable response, and apparently he'd been wrong. This did not bode well.

Sparing minimal attention for driving through the city streets, Trezini was playing chauffeur and bodyguard today; Matthew had requested Trezini's company for the morning while he attended a series of mundane appointments, making a few business-related visits along the way. The two men were virtually silent when alone together. However, Picano now stirred himself to ask, "What are you doing this afternoon?"

"You know what I'm doing," Trezini easily replied. It was unspoken but common knowledge that Matthew had had Trezini followed to his regular trysts with his lover. "Why? Do you need me for something?"

"No."

Trezini glanced over at Picano, sitting there in the passenger seat of Trezini's car. The man had been sullenly brooding all morning. What a cheerful pair they made. "Matthew? Are you going to tell me what's bothering you?"

"You didn't hear?" There was something raw about Picano's manner, which was unusual enough to worry the hell out of Trezini. Matthew said, "They arrested Genari early this morning."

"Oh God," Trezini blurted out. "They did? For killing Smith's man?"

Another miscalculation: Trezini knew his reaction had been a shade too panicked. Picano, however, seemed willing enough to let it go. "Yeah," he thoughtfully replied, "for killing Smith's man." A long moment stretched before Matthew continued, "I want to know how they narrowed it down so quickly. Even if Smith pushed the case with the cops, no one outside our inner circle knew it was Genari who pulled the trigger."

This time, Trezini did the wise thing and stayed silent. Everyone knew he was queer, sure, but he'd never been a drama queen.

"It's been obvious all along that Smith has cops on his payroll. I mean, that guy you shot in his freezer – nothing ever came of it. You'd expect Smith to at least take some flak, especially with a police officer involved."

Trezini asked, "What are you saying, Matt? What are you thinking it adds up to?"

"I don't know. Something's gone wrong somewhere. Something's not right." Picano turned to look at him, direct and … and more vulnerable than Trezini had seen him for years. "Don't you feel it?"

Staring ahead through the windshield, Trezini left as long a silence as he could.

"Cat?"

"I don't know," Trezini said, helplessly echoing the man. "I don't know."

It was obvious that Trezini wouldn't be able to get away with all this for much longer. As soon as his boss was done with him for the morning, Trezini dropped Picano off and headed home.

At first his mother was pleased, no doubt thinking Trezini must have unexpectedly found time to join her for lunch. But then she read the trouble on his face. Trezini sat her down at the kitchen table, took her hands in his, and gently said, "I'm sorry, Ma. Everything's about to change."

She whispered, "He knows?"

"He knows something's going wrong somewhere. He doesn't know what, and he doesn't know it's me yet, but he's going to figure it out soon." There were tears rolling down his mother's face; in that moment, Trezini was in great danger of crying, too. Trying to reassure her, and also trying to carefully lead up to the bad news, he said, "Matthew's an honorable man, Ma, you shouldn't be scared for yourself. But I don't want to be worrying, I need to know you're safe."

"What about you?"

"I'll have to go into hiding soon," Trezini explained, "and you could come with me, but that's no life for a lady. So I set up something with the FBI weeks ago; I got you a passport and a ticket to England in a different name." A pleading note snuck into his voice as Trezini gazed at his mother's woebegone face. *Please be okay with this.* "You can stay with those cousins you haven't seen in years. We'll tell people you've gone home to Italy, and I'm joining you there soon, and that's good cover for me." Silence for a moment. "Ma, I know you don't want to go –"

She interrupted him. "I don't care about that – of course I'll go, I knew you'd want me to. But this is goodbye now, that's what I care about."

Trezini offered her a bittersweet smile. "Yes, this is goodbye," he murmured, clutching at her hands. "Until I see you in heaven. We always knew that's where you'd be going, but now I'll be there waiting for you. All right? God's calling me to do this, Ma, so we can trust Him to take care of me."

"Yes."

"Hey, you think of me loitering around up there in a beautiful pair of wings … I'll be waiting for you, looking out for you."

"I'll pray for you, Angelo," she said, apparently long-resigned to the worst. "I'll pray for you every night and every day."

"Thank you, Ma, I'm sure He'll listen." And they sat there in silence for a while, hands wrapped up together, until Trezini got up to make them coffee.

Delaney had been watching anxiously from the window of room six. Behind him on the far side of the room, the attorney hovered and the FBI Agent paced. Though it was only quarter to two, Delaney was not surprised to hear and then see Trezini's car pull off the road and into the motel's parking lot. The man was driving so belligerently he seemed unaware that he'd almost run down someone on the sidewalk. Delaney turned and hurried out through room seven to meet him.

The car was parked haphazardly, the door was slammed closed, and Trezini was storming towards him. Delaney offered a placating hand, concerned for his lover and the whole damned situation; but Trezini brushed him away, not breaking his pace. Instead, Delaney quickly fell into step behind him.

Delaney had left the connecting door open: Trezini strode through into the other room and at last came to a halt. Valeri and Russell stood there facing him, their expressions worried and defensive. When Delaney caught up, he settled close beside Trezini, shoulder supportively overlapping shoulder.

Trezini was glaring at the other two. "Well," he said in the coldest of tones, "I think everyone here knows exactly what happened this morning." And then Trezini let fly with righteous anger. "You bastards! So you don't like me. And I wouldn't care, except you're playing with my *life*! How the hell does that compare to a *thumb*?"

Valeri tried to say, "Mr. Trezini, if you'd –"

But the man easily overrode her. "I have a job to do out there, and I don't mean managing the bar. Picano tells me to jump, I ask how high. Do you get it? I'm doing good in here –" Trezini thumped a fist against his heart, the gesture hard enough to be painful – "and I'm doing good here –" he flung an open hand around them at the room, at the transcripts scattered across the desk – "but let me tell you something: good don't play real well on the streets."

"We understand that, but –"

"But you arrested Genari!" he cried out. "I told you, you can't move on any of this until I'm someplace safe – but what do you go and do?"

It hadn't taken long for Russell's defensiveness to become an anger that almost matched Trezini's. The FBI Agent said, "Hey, *we* didn't."

Valeri quickly added, "The arrest wasn't based on your information."

Trezini, however, was too furious to hear. "Don't you realize the stakes?" And he thrust a hand back towards Delaney. "*He* didn't, in that freezer. He didn't have the first idea what he was suggesting."

The pain of that stabbed Delaney through and through again; but he grabbed Trezini's hand in his, and tried to reach him. Quietly he asked, "Angelo, please. Listen to Ms. Valeri."

And surprisingly enough, a turbulent moment of silence passed, though of course Trezini continued to glare unabated at the other two.

Valeri took a breath before beginning. "Ballistics matched the slugs in the body with a bullet from a shooting two months ago. The cops arrested Genari on both counts. They didn't know any better. I'm sorry – *we're* sorry about the pressure that puts on you, but it was completely unintentional."

Another moment passed. It was apparent that Trezini was trying to think past his fury; Delaney was pleased that Valeri and Russell gave him the room in which to do so. At last Trezini said, "He wouldn't have used the same gun. Genari would have ditched the first gun."

"Well, he didn't," said Russell, voice tightly controlled. "We have a witness who can identify Genari from the first incident – we have you telling us he killed this man – and the slugs match."

Trezini shook his head. "No. He's more careful than that. We all are."

Unable to restrain his sarcasm, Russell said, "Hey, Picano told him to jump, he asked how high. He should have asked for a clean gun."

Another moment, and Trezini's shoulders surrendered a fraction, though his tone remained hard. "Picano doesn't know about the damned bullets. Picano is assuming that someone named names. And I'm on the fucking short-list."

"We'll make it known about the slugs," Valeri assured him. "We'll make certain everyone's real clear about that."

Russell added, "All we need is some damage control."

Trezini's shoulders at last relaxed enough to resume their usual posture. "Picano's feeling uneasy anyway, he's sensed something's happening. I'm telling you now, the clock's ticking. And his idea of damage control …"

Delaney was still holding his lover's hand: he clutched it tightly for a moment, wanting to promise again: *I'll do everything I can to keep you safe. I'll do anything –*

The mobster flicked an unreadable glance back at Delaney, then turned back to consider Valeri and Russell. And Trezini announced, "I'm in no mood for you morons today."

No one bothered arguing or protesting. Valeri and Russell just watched as Trezini turned away and walked out through the connecting door. Delaney nodded a farewell and followed the man.

Trezini was moving quickly: by the time Delaney caught up, Trezini was about to open the door of his car. Delaney strode up to him, and gently rested his hand against the door's window, really nothing more than his fingertips resting there, but this lightest of gestures was enough to stop the man. Trezini waited, his head bowed, avoiding Delaney's gaze.

In the quietest tones, Delaney asked, "Are you in no mood for me?"

Eventually Trezini looked up at him; and as the man's anger further loosened its grip, it became more obvious that Trezini was scared. The two men considered each other.

And then Trezini abruptly reached up to frame Delaney's face in both hands – and he kissed him, deeply, despite the fact that they were outside in public. At first, Delaney just let this happen, seduced all too easily by Trezini's skillful and needy fervor, and willing to do anything Trezini wanted, even if it meant a world's worth of strangers seeing them. Soon, however, Delaney broke the kiss; he took Trezini's hands in his, and invited the man back to their motel room with a tilt of his head.

Trezini's face darkened. "No," he said, "not here. Not today." And the moment's passion was lost. Trezini sighed, pulled away from Delaney and got into his car. The motor rumbled and then began its expensive purr.

But then Trezini leaned forward to look up at Delaney through the windshield, and he beckoned for Delaney to join him.

Unable to suppress a smile, Delaney strode around to the passenger's side, and slid in. Trezini smoothly backed out of the parking space, and then pulled away at such a speed that Delaney was pushed back against the seat. He found himself happily surrendering.

Waiting while Trezini unlocked the back door, Delaney reflected that this was only the second time he'd visited the man's home. There was so much of his lover's life that Delaney didn't share, so many shadows he couldn't dispel. But not only that, the cop had even suggested a crusade that would eventually destroy most of the good things in Trezini's life. A crusade that Trezini was convinced would result in his own death. With these thoughts weighing on him, Delaney followed the man inside.

There was no one in the kitchen. "Ma?" Trezini called. "It's only me and Josh." There was no reply, and the house felt empty. Trezini glanced back at Delaney, and shrugged. "Maybe she's gone to church." A moment, and then he continued, "I told her it was time for her to leave, to go to England."

The man's head was lowered again – no doubt partly to avoid Delaney, but Trezini also seemed very unhappy at doing without one of the best things in his life. The fact that he'd decided to send his mother out of harm's way was ample evidence that the situation was changing.

But before Delaney could reach for the man to offer him comfort, Trezini grabbed one of his hands and led Delaney through into the house. They climbed the stairs to Trezini's bedroom and closed the door behind them. And then Delaney took charge.

He walked Trezini over to the bed and stood there facing him. Trezini
had suffered through anger and fear this afternoon; the dull aftermath looked
something like despair. Right now, what Delaney most wanted was to reach
Trezini, connect with him, cheer him – for neither man could afford to lose
hope.

Patiently, Delaney began undressing them both; alternating between an
article of his own clothing and a kiss pressed to Trezini's mouth, then a piece
of Trezini's clothing and a kiss against whatever part of the man's flesh had
been revealed. The house was quiet around them, and Trezini remained
silent, barely cooperating.

It was only once they were in the bed that Trezini began to respond, and
even then the man was passive, simply soaking up the pleasure that Delaney
had by now learned how to bestow. Moving over his lover, Delaney was
holding Trezini in his arms so that the slimmer man was arched up against
him; and Delaney was loving Trezini with all of himself, his mouth roaming
hungrily wherever it could reach. The friction of Trezini's genitals against
his own was still so shockingly intense that Delaney had begun to suspect he
would never tire of this act. It was almost as if the nerve-endings hidden in
the silky skin and aching hardness of his cock, the heavy drag of his scrotum
and the growing tightness of his balls – it was almost as if those nerve-
endings, when matched against Angelo's, created a circuit between them,
conveying an electrical current, feeding excitement to and fro in an endless
loop, building sensation …

Brightening sunshine fell across them through the lace curtains. Trezini
was moving now, participating, perhaps seeking distraction, shifting over
and under Delaney as they rolled and wrestled across the bed, each pushing
against the other as if neither would ever get close enough to his lover no
matter how hard he tried.

And then Trezini shattered through some internal barrier, rediscovering
peace, losing his troubles in the shared passion. Once more he surrendered,
became passive, let Delaney work over him; but this time Trezini was
suffused with joy, not despair. He was lying back in the center of the bed,
his arms stretched wide and his legs together, echoing the crucifix on the
wall above them. Delaney's arms were cradling Trezini's shoulders again,
and his legs were spread either side of Trezini's, and he was thrusting himself
in gentle rhythm against the man. This was beautiful, thoroughly beautiful.

Indistinct words in a reverent tone, slowly becoming clearer until at last Delaney realized that Trezini was murmuring their psalm. "Thou preparest a table before me in the presence of mine enemies; Thou anointest my head with oil; My cup runneth over. Surely goodness and mercy shall follow me; All the days of my … life …"

The words faltered as Trezini lost himself further in a quietly profound orgasm. Semen welled between them. Delaney watched the man lovingly, maintaining the tender caress of body against body, feeling rather pleased with himself for achieving so much.

Eventually, those green-hazel eyes opened, and they stared up at Delaney, full of trust, perhaps a little curious. Could this clever lover of Trezini's really be Joshua Delaney, not so long ago the least imaginative of men? Delaney was a mystery to himself these days. At times, a delightful mystery. And perhaps he was a mystery to Trezini, too, for a hint of doubt now crossed the man's face. Delaney let out a quiet laugh, whispering, "Angelo."

"I underestimated you," Trezini confessed in a whisper.

"My ability? You teach me, inspire me."

"Your … generosity. How blind I've been."

"I'm only as generous as the next man." Delaney was still moving in the golden glow of utter contentment. "Can we do this forever?"

"No."

"No?"

Trezini was smiling, beautiful and indulgent. "No, Josh, because any moment now you're going to come –" Delaney shivered, just hearing the words – "and you won't let your eyes close because I'll be watching you, and you'll be watching me, and we'll share every last ounce of your pleasure together …"

"Yes," Delaney whispered, and they did exactly that.

Matthew Picano sat at his desk, completely cool and collected, listening to one of Smith's thugs tell tales. The guy stood before him, nervous, glancing back over his shoulder every now and then at two of Picano's men loitering in the shadows on the far side of the room. It was really too late in the evening to be bothering over this petty stuff.

"Oh, *please*," Picano soon interrupted. "I know Mr. Trezini is gay. I know he's seeing some married guy. I know they rendezvous at the Comfort Inn."

"*That's* where I saw him, this afternoon," the thug broke in, too scared to be wise. "I was walking along the sidewalk, I stopped to light a cigarette, and he almost ran me down. I wouldn't have noticed him otherwise. Looked like he was really pissed off about something."

Picano lifted his eyes to heaven, praying for patience. "Your information isn't worth terribly much. Is it really a peace offering –"

"Yes. Of course."

"– or is your boss trying to turn me against one of my own people? Tell Mr. Smith that I don't see the issue here. Mr. Trezini and his friend are consenting adults, and I really don't give a damn what they get up to in the privacy of their own hotel room."

The man was silent, though it seemed he had more to say.

Picano commented, "If Mr. Smith thinks my employment practices are too broad, then perhaps it's time he took a reality check."

At last the thug blurted out, "You know the other guy's name is Joshua Delaney?"

"Yes," Picano said, though so far he'd only gotten the first name.

"You know Delaney used to be a cop?"

Ah. Picano carefully did not react. The answer was obviously no. It was just as well he hadn't given in to the temptation to spiel about how honest and trustworthy Carmine Trezini was despite his odd proclivities. Picano appeared quite foolish enough for now.

The thug was continuing, "Look, Mr. Picano, I was one of the guys who put your man Trezini in Mr. Smith's freezer."

That helped explain why the guy was so nervous about being here. Picano had never publicly forgiven Smith for that.

"Well, Delaney showed up at the warehouse that same night and I put him in there with Mr. Trezini. Delaney was wearing a uniform. I did some asking around this afternoon, and I'm told Delaney resigned a couple of days later. They said it's not clear why."

Picano decided it was time to take charge of the conversation again, especially as he'd recovered enough to be sarcastic. "No doubt Mr. Delaney resigned in order to concentrate on his new writing career, and to spend more time with Mr. Trezini – and who could blame him? Thank you, but I remain unimpressed by your boss's gesture."

A long moment stretched. Apparently the thug had no further information to pass on. He tried, "And I should tell Mr. Smith that … ?"

"That I'm unimpressed," Picano repeated.

The impatient dismissal was obvious. Smith's thug accepted the message with misgivings; he nodded a respectful farewell, and headed for the door. One of Picano's men accompanied him out of the house.

Once they'd reassembled in the office, Picano stood up to give his orders. "Have someone watch the hotel next time Trezini meets this guy. Be tactful about it, be clever. See if they do anything more than fuck." He took a breath, leaned forward with both hands on the desk, and then met his men's gazes directly. "But it's Cat, after all, and Smith's still a moron – don't do anything without checking back with me. All right?"

"Yes, Mr. Picano." And the two of them left.

Picano sank back down into his chair with a frown, torn over whether to dismiss the matter. Delaney being an ex-cop – or even if he'd still been a cop – didn't necessarily mean he was on the wrong side. As for Trezini, his loyalties had always been too personal for an easy change. And, after all, how much trouble was the man really capable of causing? "It's only Cat," Picano muttered to himself in the darkness. "He has a conscience, but it's only Cat."

Somewhat less than forty-eight hours later, Picano was being given a little more information – one of his low-level thugs was reporting to him while Picano sat there maintaining the blankest of expressions. He'd sent Genari out of the room, not wanting anyone else to hear this until Picano had formed his own opinion.

"Mr. Trezini was in that room from two o'clock until four," the thug was saying. "Delaney was already there when he arrived."

"That's their routine," Picano observed impatiently.

"Yes, Mr. Picano, but I hung around after Mr. Trezini had left, and there was something odd." The man shrugged as if he wasn't sure how much importance to attach to this. "Delaney went inside again after watching Mr. Trezini go, and then he came out a few minutes later – and at pretty much the same time this couple came out of the room next door. The guy was in a grey suit, he looked just like a Fed, and they were both carrying files and briefcases and stuff."

"Well, and did Delaney know them?"

"No, I don't think so, they didn't even look at each other, but the timing was kind of suspicious. So I talked to the guy at reception. Cagey bastard said it was none of his business what Mr. Trezini was using his room for. Live and let live, he said, so long as Mr. Trezini paid for it. The room, I mean. Then the guy said the couple next door were attending a conference but he wouldn't tell me which one, and he wouldn't say how long they were staying for."

"Is that it?" Picano demanded. And he let out a disgusted noise when the man nodded. None of this was conclusive, one way or the other, though Matthew was becoming less and less inclined to make excuses for his old pal. Even this thug of his could spot a Fed when he saw one. Picano stood, and yelled out, "Two days go by, and that's all you've got?"

"Sorry, Mr. Picano," the guy mumbled.

"Get out of here!"

Alone again, Picano sat down. Something was going wrong somewhere, and he had his suspicions, that was all, there were no actual facts as yet – but Matthew could no longer avoid the idea that Cat might be betraying him. It hurt. Just in that moment, Matthew could admit it hurt like hell. After all that they'd been through together over the years, after all Picano had done for the man, after all he'd put up with on Trezini's behalf … Matthew had treated Cat fairly, even favored him, when other people wouldn't have given him the time of day. And how did Cat repay that debt?

Well, if this had been Matthew's father discovering that his right-hand man might have betrayed him, Trezini's father wouldn't have been long for this world. But Picano had come a long way since those days. Picano ran his business a little differently now.

He waited a while, sitting there on his own; he waited until the edge of the hurt had dulled, and the heat of the fury had cooled … and then he reached for the phone.

Trezini was at Carmine's, as usual, ensuring that everything was running smoothly on this busy Friday night. People came here for the subtle first-class service and while he was proud of his staff, Trezini knew that his presence helped set the tone and ease everything along. Right now, he was behind the bar preparing two Manhattans and providing amiable conversation for a customer, while his bartenders bustled discreetly and efficiently around him. The front door opened, Trezini glanced up – and he was surprised to see Joshua Delaney walking in.

Pleasure followed quickly on the heels of surprise. For the sake of maintaining their cover, Delaney had never visited the bar, and Trezini welcomed the chance to show the place off to his lover.

However, as Delaney strode calmly and purposefully towards Trezini, the pleasure was forgotten – this could only mean one thing and Trezini had been remarkably slow in not reaching that conclusion sooner. Trezini excused himself to the customer, told him the drinks were on the house, collected his jacket and walked out from behind the bar to meet Delaney.

A loving and protective hand settled in the small of his back, and Trezini was escorted towards the door. None of the staff or customers – in fact, no one but he and Delaney realized that Trezini was leaving his day-to-day life behind forever. It was a disconcerting notion, one that he felt he should have been better prepared for.

The phone rang and Trezini glanced back to see one of the bartenders pick it up. A moment later the young man called, "Mr. Trezini! Sir, it's for you."

And everything indicated that it was Matthew Picano calling – everything from Delaney's presence to the bartender's wary, urgent manner.

Trezini paused and turned to give the bartender a reassuring smile. As Delaney hovered at his shoulder, Trezini calmly said, "Tell him I have a hot date with Joshua, and I'll call him back."

Three more steps and Delaney, ever the gentleman, held the door open for Trezini. The mobster checked around for Picano's goons, but there were none. It seemed he and Delaney had escaped – presumably the pair of them were safe for now … And nothing would ever be the same again.

CHAPTER SEVEN

Trezini was looking a little stunned. Delaney kept an eye on him while dialing the phone: the man was sitting there on the shabby sofa in his elegant expensive suit, looking completely out of place in the joyless urban safe-house. Even this living room, the most open area in the house, was cramped. Full-length windows looked onto a tiny enclosed paved area, but that only served to emphasize that they were shut away from the world.

The phone was answered on the first ring. "Yes?"

"Ms. Valeri, it's Joshua Delaney –"

"You picked him up?"

Delaney almost smiled at her impatient concern. "Yes, I've brought Mr. Trezini to the safe-house. He's fine and I don't believe we alerted anyone."

"Good."

"You have the necessary warrants?" he asked, curious. Well, if the truth were known, curious and resentful at being left on the sidelines.

"Yes, we're ready to roll – so I've got to go, all right?"

"Of course."

Nevertheless, Valeri paused for a moment. And then she said, "Take care of him, Joshua."

"Yes, I will," he replied politely, "thank you. Goodnight, ma'am." Delaney hung up, and then sat down beside Trezini, not touching the man. A moment stretched as they both considered the situation.

Eventually Trezini dully asked, "You had this place set up already?"

"Yes. There had to be somewhere I could take you, in case things went wrong." Delaney looked at the man. "I'm sorry. You deserve better than to live like this. But the house is secure, and very few people know about it."

Trezini seemed uninterested; he'd barely looked around since they got here, and he didn't comment now. Instead he asked, "So, what went wrong?"

"The clerk at the motel was being asked questions by someone we can only assume works for Matthew Picano. And he wasn't only interested in us – he was asking about the people in room six. The clerk called Ms. Valeri."

Another moment dragged by. "What happens next?" Trezini asked.

"You and I wait here," Delaney announced, "while Agent Russell arrests Mr. Picano and his associates."

That sparked a reaction. Trezini turned to him in surprise. "They're ready to take the case to court?"

"No. But it's best for you if we make this public now."

"Oh."

The two of them subsided into silence and then they just sat there some more. Events were moving and all Trezini and Delaney could do was wait, though neither man liked the notion. Delaney figured he had the advantage, though, in that he was used to being marginalized, while Trezini was accustomed to being in the thick of whatever was going on.

Eventually, Delaney reached to hold Trezini's hand in his, offering the reassurance of companionship. And they waited.

Picano had called Genari back to his office, and he'd summoned Bacchelli, another member of his inner circle – and then Jonathan Howe the accountant had turned up for his regular weekly session with the boss. So now Genari and Bacchelli, these two self-satisfied high-level mobsters, were sitting there wondering why on earth they were included in a mundane financial meeting. Yes, they were puzzled, but they weren't questioning him. No one ever questioned Picano, no one would dare, except of course Cat when the occasion demanded it. Trezini had been faithful to Picano's best interests for so damned long now.

But sooner or later, once the accountant was gone and his profit-and-loss statements with him, Picano was going to have to say, *There's something going wrong somewhere, and I think it's Cat.* He needed to get this checked out and Genari would have to do it, he was the one who knew most about the local cops. Picano wondered what Trezini's hot date might entail that resulted in this change in the lovers' routine. Could it be something as simple and harmless and personal as Delaney turning his back on his wife for Cat after all? Or was it something more sinister?

It was difficult to concentrate on business with these questions plaguing him. Finally, Howe was tidying his reports and statements away, tucking all the paperwork into his leather briefcase. Picano was left with no clear idea of the state of his finances but took it for granted that they were disgustingly healthy.

There was a firm knock at the front door.

Picano found himself startled, having not expected any further visitors that night. This might be trouble – and trouble at this moment could be serious. He sat there listening, not moving, while the others bustled around, oblivious.

High heels tapping across the slate; Nicola had gone to answer the door. Her voice was too quiet for Picano to hear. He could just make out a man talking to her, his tones polite but determined.

And then Nicola was bringing the man to Picano's office, and the heavy footsteps following the tap-tap-tap indicated there were a number of people out there.

Picano stood up from his chair as Nicola opened the door; his first impression was of her pretty face soured with worry. And then some guy who was obviously a federal agent strode in, warrants in hand, with more agents and police officers at his shoulders. The crowd of them swarmed around the room but Picano just waited, staring at the first man.

Identifying himself as Agent Edgar Russell, the guy proceeded to handcuff Picano, list the charges, and read him his rights. Picano remained cool, though he figured he was probably betraying a shade of bitterness. He'd been too slow. Because it was Cat, because it was Carmine Trezini, Matthew had doubted and hesitated, and that might prove to be far more trouble than the friendship had been worth. Foolish. Very foolish.

The other FBI agents were arresting Genari and Bacchelli and Howe. Sensibly, they all stayed silent, though the mobsters were brimming over with anger while the accountant quaked in trepidation.

Poor Nicola was watching all this from the doorway. Once he was done with Picano, Russell cast a speculative glance her way. Picano spoke for the first time: "Leave her alone, she has nothing to do with this." And the FBI agent nodded acquiescence.

No one else was showing any respect. The other agents and the police officers – Picano wondered how many of them he'd invested in, and whether that would affect the outcome – the others were seizing anything and everything in the office that might be evidence. The computer was taken and the boxes of floppy discs; files and account books and Howe's briefcase; the strongbox from the desk that contained Picano's rather generous cash float; the two hand-guns he had in the desk drawers. Everything.

But surely this wasn't anything Picano couldn't get out of. He'd been doing business in this town for a long time; he had the name and the influence to ride this out. After all, as Matthew had reflected before, just how much trouble could Cat cause?

Denise Valeri accompanied the FBI agents and police officers who were invading Carmine's bar; at the same time, teams throughout the West Side were raiding a selection of Matthew Picano's other businesses and the attached gambling dens, and Russell was arresting the mob boss himself.

The bar's quiet stylish atmosphere was brutally disturbed as uniformed officers and flak-jacketed agents strode in. Staff and patrons were ordered to remain exactly where they were, to not touch or move anything – and they obeyed, most of them too shocked to comprehend what was happening.

Angry protesting cries could be heard from the next room, though. One of the FBI agents kicked open the door hidden away at the end of the bar, and Valeri hurried across to peer over his shoulder at the gambling den. Another team had broken into the den through a back door, effectively preventing the flight of both staff and gamblers.

A thug, presumably one of Picano's, instinctively drew his weapon – and everyone but the law enforcement officers sensibly ducked. Within moments, the thug was subdued by sheer force of numbers.

With the bar and gambling den successfully secured, the agents and the officers settled into routine as best they could, despite the adrenalin rush taking its own sweet time to ease. Valeri assumed that similar tasks were being undertaken in three other West Side establishments: a laundromat, a restaurant and another bar. Everyone present would be questioned; evidence from the gambling dens would be seized. Valeri watched as piles of cash and decks of playing cards were photographed *in situ* and then bagged, along with roulette wheels and poker machines and other gambling paraphernalia.

Of course, the bartenders and the croupiers and the gamblers all knew what was going on, but many of the bar's customers – the people who'd simply come to have a drink and while the evening away at Carmine's – had no idea. No doubt it was the same at Picano's other establishments: right now, there would be law-abiding people interrupted in washing their clothes at the laundromat or eating their dinners at Cin Cin. Valeri oversaw the process as such patrons were quickly cleared and released – their names and addresses having been confirmed through their driver's licenses or other identification, and recorded.

And then the FBI agents began interviewing the staff, one-to-one, using the booths and scattered tables. This was a move calculated to take advantage of their shaken state. Nevertheless, as Valeri wandered from pair to pair, she found that the bartenders and croupiers were either too loyal or too scared to admit to having anything to do with Matthew Picano. They all kept a wary eye on each other, perhaps wondering if anyone would crack.

The police officers had nothing much to do for the moment. They gathered around the bar itself – and after a bit of mutual encouragement, they began munching on the complimentary bowls of nuts and crackers. Eventually, one of them even headed around behind the bar and began pouring glasses of coke. Seeing this, the agents rolled their eyes in exasperation but no one bothered preventing them, and Valeri figured it wasn't worth her while.

When it appeared that nothing further could be gained by the on-the-spot interviews, the staff directly involved in the gambling den were arrested and taken out to the police vans. The last of the evidence was bagged and catalogued. The rooms were photographed once more. One of the FBI agents stood there surveying this bustle of professional activity and offered Valeri a satisfied nod. It seemed this raid had been a success.

Valeri was the last to leave. Carmine's bar felt forlorn now, empty but for the detritus of an interrupted evening.

Once she'd stepped outside, a police officer knelt to fasten a heavy padlock across the front doors – the padlock looked crass next to the elegant gold door handles and the screws had damaged the polished wood. Crime-scene tape disfigured everything. Valeri let out a silent sigh, and hoped that Trezini wouldn't have to see the place like this; she feared he'd be heartbroken.

Trezini said sadly, "I really loved that bar, you know. I never expected to love it when Matt first gave it to me, but I did."

When Trezini didn't get an immediate response, he looked over at Delaney. They were both loitering on and around the sofa of the safe-house, passing time. The cop was as restless as the mobster, which perhaps wasn't unexpected on this their third day in captivity – however, Delaney had always seemed so self-contained before, a haven of stillness whether peaceful or thoughtful. Eventually, the man asked, "Is that what you'll do when this is over? Manage a bar of your own?"

That deserved a snort of laughter but Trezini restrained himself. Instead he replied, "Josh my love, I doubt there are any bars in heaven."

And Trezini was glad he hadn't laughed because Delaney turned to him with a hurt expression on his face. It seemed the man was surprised to find that Trezini still assumed he'd be killed.

Taking pity on him, Trezini redirected the conversation. "Hey, what will you do afterwards? They'll promote you to Detective, right? At the very least. Or maybe the FBI will make you an offer. Like the Lieutenant said, your careers will all go into orbit."

"No, mine won't," Delaney said quietly.

Trezini frowned. "You've proved yourself; you're a good cop, Josh, and I know what I'm talking about. Why don't you try for Internal Affairs? You came here because you turned in your own people, after all."

Delaney seemed to have difficulty getting his reply out. "I asked them once. They told me I'm too naive." Perhaps this had caused him pain in the past.

"Well," Trezini asked, "and are you?"

"I don't know." A shrug of those broad shoulders. "I've seen so many things, good and bad. I haven't led a sheltered life."

"Then, how come people still call you naive?"

"I don't know," was the helpless response.

Delaney was saved from Trezini's further interrogation by the front door bell ringing. The cop walked over to check a small security monitor that displayed an image of the house's enclosed entrance. He announced, "It's Ms. Valeri and Agent Russell," and he buzzed them in, continuing to watch the monitor carefully.

A moment later, Valeri and Russell walked into the room, both of them looking tired. Trezini found himself pathetically glad to see them, eager for any contact with the outside world. He asked, "How's it going out there?"

Valeri sank to sit on the sofa. "My God, where do I start? My boss and I got carpeted by the Mayor this morning. Apparently, he didn't think we'd go so far as to actually make an arrest."

Trezini let out a laugh and said, "The guy's scared that Picano will take him down, too."

It was almost comical how the three law enforcement people reacted to this idea. Startled, they exchanged wary looks with each other, before Valeri carefully asked, "Mr. Trezini, are you suggesting corruption at that level?"

"No, don't get too excited," Trezini replied. "I can't help you there. But with Picano being intrinsic to Chicago for so long, there must have been compromises made along the way. This will affect a whole lot of people, you might get some surprises."

Valeri nodded, and let this one go. "Well, anyway, so there's the Prosecuting Attorney and me sitting before the Mayor's desk, and he's pacing back and forth all over the room, talking and gesturing. He was angry."

"What about, exactly?" Delaney prompted.

"You know he's up for re-election soon? His campaign is going to be based around promising to clean up the city, but focusing on drugs. And that's reasonable; I mean, who can argue with that? But the Mayor doesn't appreciate us targeting other high-profile crimes right now."

"It distracts people's attention," Russell added.

Valeri continued, "The thing is, when he was done yelling at us, when he was shaking our hands and telling us we were doing a fine job but we just need to review our priorities – he said to remember that it's better the devil you know."

The four of them all looked at each other, wondering how to interpret this. One by one they had come to join Valeri, so they were all sitting around the coffee table by now, at the same level.

Valeri repeated thoughtfully, "It's better the devil you know …"

Trezini asked the obvious rhetorical question, "So, how well does he know this particular devil?"

"For that matter, who's the devil we don't know?"

"He didn't actually tell you to quit?" Russell asked. When Valeri shook her head in the negative, he continued, "Then I guess we just keep watching for the fallout. Like you said, Trezini, we might be surprised."

That was more direct acknowledgement than Trezini had gotten before from this man; but he didn't deign to draw attention to that fact, with either surprise or gratitude. He felt a slight sense of relief, however, to know that his reliance on the FBI Agent wasn't too badly misplaced.

Delaney asked, "What else is happening?"

"We're still interviewing the people we arrested the other night," Valeri said, "and doing background checks. It won't be long and we'll be ready to take the whole thing to a grand jury to seek indictments against Picano." She let out a sigh. "Except every day seems to bring as many questions as answers."

"Such as?" Trezini prompted.

"Who's Jonathan Howe?"

Trezini almost smiled at this news. "You got him? That's good."

"Yes, he was at Picano's house on the night of the raid. But Howe isn't being very forthcoming. What's his role in all this?"

"He's good with money," Trezini informed her, "but not much else. He shouldn't be too tough a nut for you to crack."

"Hold on a moment," Valeri said, reluctantly shifting. She dragged out the tape recorder from her box of files and other assorted objects; Delaney rose to go plug it in to the nearest electrical outlet. "Okay, Mr. Trezini," she said, after she'd gone through the usual details and identifications, "tell us about Jonathan Howe."

Denise Valeri stood to one side of the witness stand, deliberately not drawing attention to herself by tone or gesture: Carmine Angelo Trezini was testifying before the grand jury, and he not only deserved center stage but seemed to instinctively command it. He was going to make a great witness at the trial and would need very little coaching.

Grand juries were notoriously inattentive. Valeri had occasionally presented prosecution cases to jury members who sat there openly reading novels, knitting, doing crossword puzzles, even sleeping. This time, though, the atmosphere was different. The jury was interested and mostly awake. That might be because they'd only recently been empaneled, or it might be due to Matthew Picano being the defendant. Or it might be that Trezini was not only easy to listen to, but he was presenting some fascinating material.

The small wood-lined room was quiet; a few high windows let dusty light in to shine on Trezini. Continuing her practice of keeping her questions brief, but broad in focus, Valeri now asked the man, "Who is Jonathan Howe?"

"Mr. Howe is Mr. Picano's financial adviser. He'd be able to tell you exactly how Mr. Picano handled all the cash – the dodges they used, the ways they laundered it, where they invested it. There was a *lot* of cash coming in through the gambling dens, believe me, so Mr. Howe needed to deal with that behind the scenes; they needed to avoid questions from the authorities. I only really know how it worked at Carmine's, the bar I ran, but Mr. Picano set up all his businesses much the same way."

"All right, Mr. Trezini, would you tell us how it worked at your bar?" Valeri knew this by heart, of course – she could virtually give the testimony herself – but she maintained a professionally interested demeanor, and Trezini told the tale anew with no hesitation. The grand jury drank it all in as if each and every member had been thirsty for years.

Trezini loosened the knot of his tie, then sank down into the depths of the uncomfortable sofa and closed his eyes, ignoring Valeri and Russell.

"I'm not surprised you're tired," Valeri commented from across the coffee table. "Testifying is exhausting work."

But it was crazy, really: Trezini was doing far less than he was accustomed to these days, he was juggling far fewer balls than he'd once been responsible for; why should he find this new life so draining?

Delaney walked through from the tiny kitchen, a tray of mismatched mugs and coffee fixings in his competent hands. The man tactfully directed the topic of conversation away from Trezini by asking, "And how are you, Ms. Valeri? I should think you're far busier than we are."

"I'm holding up," she replied. Trezini lifted one eyelid just far enough to see her smiling up at Delaney, charmed by his genuine concern. Well, Trezini knew how that felt; he'd been thoroughly enthralled by this man for weeks. Unfortunately, Valeri must have decided that the minimal movement was a sign of life, for she returned her attention to Trezini. "I have to warn you that the grand jury is only the beginning, Mr. Trezini. You'll be going over this same information a hundred times before we're done."

"I know," Trezini murmured. Like they hadn't done that already. "It'll be fine."

"And when we *are* done –" Valeri was relentless – "we'll need to get you into the Witness Protection Program. You should start thinking about where you might want to live, what kind of work you'd like."

Trezini turned his face away, shrugging this off, having thought Valeri was smarter than that.

He was left in peace while the other three drank their coffee, carrying on a desultory commonplace conversation as if Trezini wasn't there. Eventually, Valeri and Russell got up and prepared to leave.

Delaney stood, too, and began accompanying them towards the front door. However, halfway there the man paused and said, "You asked me to resign from the Police Department. Am I officially reinstated now?"

"I believe so," Valeri said.

"Would you make sure?" the cop persisted.

Russell asked, "Thinking of your career, Delaney?"

"No. If anything happens, I want to know that I'm acting as a law enforcement officer."

Trezini opened his eyes at this bald statement. The three of them were standing there staring soberly at each other, as Delaney's meaning sunk in. Perhaps this was a timely reminder for the others that something tragic could and indeed would happen. Eventually Valeri and Russell nodded their understanding, and then they left.

The two men were alone again, and it was apparent they were both feeling restless and dissatisfied. Trezini stirred himself to find the remote and turn the television on, and he disconsolately surfed the channels; but he found nothing worthwhile so eventually he turned it off again.

Silence. At last Trezini said, "I'm going crazy with boredom, but that's not a good enough reason to make love to you."

Delaney immediately said, "I can think of several better reasons." And the man held out his hand.

It was his left hand – and for the first time since Delaney brought him to the safe-house, Trezini noticed that Delaney was still wearing his father's wedding band. And there was no real reason for him to do so, because they didn't need it for their cover anymore. Well, no reason other than that – crusades aside – Delaney actually harbored some genuine affection for Trezini.

Knowing he was grinning like the happiest of idiots, Trezini stood and went to meet his lover's embrace.

CHAPTER EIGHT

Delaney accompanied Trezini to court each day. In fact, Delaney barely let Trezini out of his sight *ever*, though he endeavored to be as unobtrusive about this as possible; he didn't want to get in Trezini's way, and he didn't want the man to tire of him.

For safety's sake, they travelled to and from the house in the back of an enclosed van, with the same amiable driver every day and nothing to look at but each other. Neither man had been outside, not properly, for a few weeks now.

Today Trezini commented, "It's *so* nice to get out of the house." And his tone was wry because even though they remained confined within four walls, at least the walls were different and that in itself was something to be thankful for.

Upon arriving at the courthouse, the van passed through a security gate and the driver took them down into the basement parking lot. They were dropped off right by the elevators and then made their own way up into the building.

Deputy Prosecuting Attorney Valeri was waiting for them outside the grand jury room, carrying her usual files. As Trezini and Delaney walked over to her, the cop maintained a careful watch on everyone and everything around them, though there were few people in the halls and none of them were paying any attention to Trezini. A security guard stood outside the grand jury room, due to the nature of this case; nevertheless, Delaney wasn't willing to take any chances.

Greeting them with a smile, Valeri said, "It's your last day of grand jury testimony, Mr. Trezini; then we'll ask for the indictments. And they're going to say yes."

"Hallelujah," Trezini intoned.

"You've done well," the woman told him, before turning to lead the way inside.

This was one place where Delaney had to let Trezini out of his sight: no one but the witness, the prosecuting attorney and the jury members were allowed inside; not even security. Before following Valeri, Trezini pressed a farewell kiss to Delaney's cheek, which Delaney calmly accepted. He had become resigned to this kind of behavior in public from his demonstrative lover. If the truth were told, Delaney was actually kind of charmed by it, now that he'd gotten over his initial embarrassment.

All Delaney could do for the moment was wait. Since he'd begun living in the safe-house, he'd formed a new habit, in which he now indulged: Delaney wandered over to stand by the nearest window, despite the glass being opaque. He didn't like being shut away inside and this was the closest he could come to subverting the situation. The confinement was something he endured, for Trezini's sake.

The windows of the safe-house's living area were full-length, but it only revealed a tiny walled-in paved area, with a patch of sky above. The next room along – Delaney and Trezini's bedroom – was arranged in exactly the same way. But Delaney supposed a scrap of outside space was better than nothing; even on a day like today when lowering clouds increased the gloom.

Delaney was standing there looking out through the living room window while Valeri, Russell and Trezini sat behind him at the coffee table, working over a pile of transcripts and files. Christine Eliot, Delaney's boss, was there, too. Once she'd gotten tired of listening to the detail of Valeri's court strategy, Eliot came over to stand with Delaney.

Indicating a nearby carton containing newspapers, books and videos, Eliot said, "I brought you some stuff. Will this keep you entertained?"

"Yes, thank you." Delaney offered her a smile. "I'm a simple man, Lieutenant, it doesn't take much to content me."

Eliot laughed. "No, only *him*," she said, aiming a throwaway gesture at Trezini. "And he's not simple."

"Well, no, he's not," Delaney agreed, considering this notion but unwilling to discuss it.

A pause, then Eliot observed, "The isolation must be driving you nuts."

"I'm all right."

"Really?"

Delaney nodded, for it was the truth. It wasn't the lack of company that worried him; he was used to being alone though he could understand Eliot's doubts, and he was comfortable living with Trezini. But it was a significant change for Trezini, perhaps too much for the man to bear for long. Delaney found himself quietly blurting out, "This is hardest on Angelo. He had his mother, the staff and customers at Carmine's. He was part of Picano's inner circle. Angelo spent his whole life trying to get into the in-crowd, but I don't think he realized he was so … intrinsic to his neighborhood until he lost it all."

"He didn't lose it," Eliot said; "he chose to turn away from them."

"It was his decision and it was the best decision he could make. But that doesn't mean the consequences are easy to live with."

Eliot was considering him with some interest. After a moment she asked, "You really care about him, don't you? I mean, it's obvious he thinks you're the romance of the century, but you've really come to care for him."

Uncomfortable with such observations, Delaney said, "Mr. Trezini deserves to be cared about." And that was the truth, too, even though it was expressed in horribly stilted tones.

"You're a good man, Joshua."

"And so is he," Delaney muttered. Desperately seeking a change of topic, Delaney knelt by the carton of goodies and began looking through them. "Thank you for bringing this."

"Least I could do."

To his great surprise, amidst the novels and the movies, Delaney discovered a box of condoms tucked away in the bottom of the carton. He hauled it out and stared at the box with some confusion.

Eliot simply said, "Trezini asked for them."

Delaney remained too flummoxed to respond.

"Joshua …" When he looked up, he saw that Eliot was torn between laughing and frowning. "Christ," she exclaimed, "you do know about safe sex, don't you?"

"Ah, yes," Delaney stuttered out, "but we …" He swallowed, tried again, "Well, of course …" and failed miserably.

At Delaney's obvious mortification, Eliot opted for bursting into laughter. The others looked over to see what was so funny. And – though Eliot's hilarity wasn't unkind, and though the others wouldn't know why she was laughing – Delaney wanted nothing more than for the earth to swallow him whole. Outside, it began to rain.

Delaney pulled a meal together, even more haphazard than his usual attempts, and he and Trezini ate it while watching one of the videos. The rain poured down outside, so relentlessly that it seemed it would never end. Inside, the two men were silent but for the most necessary and minimal of exchanges.

Eventually, once the movie had finished and the tape was rewinding, Delaney went to fetch the box of condoms. He put it on the coffee table, and stood there waiting while Trezini stared at it for a moment and then looked up at Delaney. Apparently, Trezini wasn't embarrassed by this and he certainly didn't become defensive. It seemed, instead, that Trezini was waiting for something; perhaps for Delaney's reaction.

Given that Trezini wasn't going to speak, Delaney at last cleared his throat and said, "What, er – what were you intending?"

A wry smile twisted the man's lips. "You mean who's going to do what to whom?"

"Yes."

Trezini looked up at him some more, and then dropped his gaze towards the blank television. Oh-so-lightly he commented, "There go my grand seduction plans."

"Just tell me."

"You want to hear it plain and simple? You want to cut right to the chase?" When Trezini lifted his face towards him again, Delaney nodded once, firmly. "Well, then," Trezini announced: "I want to have you."

This wasn't such a surprise, though Delaney felt an odd sense of relief now that he knew for sure.

"What do you say, Josh?"

It took a moment for him to relocate his voice. "All right," Delaney answered when he could.

Trezini stared up at him, apparently surprised. "All right? Just like that?" He stood, and drew closer. "Did I miscalculate, Josh? Maybe I didn't need any seduction plans, maybe I didn't need to take it slow, maybe I didn't need to convince you." Trezini was with him now, winding his arms around Delaney's waist, pressing his slim sensual body up against Delaney's stockier frame. "Maybe I underestimated you yet again …"

And they were kissing, Trezini already abandoning himself to the strength of his passion. After a moment, Delaney surrendered to the flow of sensation. It wasn't that he didn't feel trepidation; it was more that he wanted to meet his lover's need despite his own doubts and fears. He trusted that Trezini would make it good for him – or at least as good as it could be.

Trezini broke away to say, "Come to bed."

"Soon," Delaney promised, disentangling himself. Trezini wouldn't quite let him go, so Delaney took the man with him over to the security monitors.

"What?" Trezini seemed astounded. "Even now, even tonight, even in the middle of all this, you're double-checking the security systems?"

"I check them every night," Delaney said, as steadily as he could. Actually, the routine was a redundancy, as he always ensured everything was functional and secure immediately after their visitors left, but Delaney was nothing if not careful.

"*God*, Josh." When Delaney turned his head to meet Trezini's gaze, the man said, "*God*, I love you."

Having completed his task, Delaney gathered Angelo Trezini up in his arms, and kissed him. The passion was, by now, intense and utterly mutual.

Delaney was lying face-down on the bed, his head twisted to one side. Through the bedroom's full-length window, he could see the rain bucketing down into the tiny paved area outside. Everything was in darkness. And Trezini was moving over him, moving within him. Completely wrung out by now, Delaney whispered, "Angelo … Angelo, please."

Trezini had taken his time with this, he'd taken it slow. Delaney supposed he should be grateful for that, as Trezini's patience had ensured this act was as easy for Delaney as possible. Nevertheless, Delaney was ashamed to admit that he simply wanted it to be over. Trezini's breathing was sharp, deep, and he was moaning a little in the unknowing way that meant he was deep in sensation. Not long now.

The open box of condoms was sitting there discarded on the bedside chest of drawers, along with a tube of lubricant. Delaney stared at it – until a distant flash of lightning distracted him, a rumble of thunder adding its punctuation. The rain abruptly increased in intensity, which hardly seemed possible for it had already been a deluge – and there was a closer flash of lightning. Thunder crashed overhead as Delaney again pleaded, "Angelo!"

All was quiet under the storm's battering. Delaney stood naked by the bedroom window, staring at the falling rain, lost in quiet contemplation of what he'd just done. Oddly enough, despite having had a male lover throughout these few months, it seemed as if an irrevocable step had only now been taken. Delaney couldn't find it in him, however, to regret it.

Behind him, Trezini was asleep, lying back on the bed in a satisfied, attractive sprawl. Delaney turned to consider him, pondering the complexities of the man, mulling over all of Trezini's mysteries that Delaney didn't want to ever solve. The cop was still utterly fascinated by the repentant mobster.

Thunder rumbled, so loud that it seemed directly above the house. A moment later, Delaney realized there had been another sound, almost hidden by the weather. He glanced up, and there it was again – the barest ominous whisper of a footfall in the roof area. This was no doubt what Trezini had feared all along; at least, Delaney couldn't afford to assume otherwise.

Silently and quickly, Delaney walked over to the bed – he woke Trezini, and pressed a finger to Trezini's lips, indicating that he should be quiet. Survival instincts forever alert, Trezini immediately realized that something must be wrong, and he took a moment to shake the sleep away. They each picked up their handguns, and checked the weapons were loaded.

Delaney leaned over to press the alarm button located near the bed-head – it alerted the police and the FBI directly. He didn't activate the alarm that would ring within the safe-house itself because he thought it would be best for Trezini to simply slip quietly away, without alerting their attackers.

Keeping their guns close to hand, both men began pulling on the clothes that lay scattered on the floor. Each ended up wearing an assortment of his own clothes and his lover's, but neither had the time or inclination to sort that out.

There was another sound – this time from the front of the house. Apparently someone had bypassed the security system and was coming in through the front door. Hearing this, Delaney came to a different decision on what to do. He unlocked the bedroom window and slid it partially open, then he picked up the bedside drawers and climbed outside into the tiny courtyard. He placed the drawers at the foot of the wall, which would otherwise be too high for either man to easily scale, and he beckoned Trezini to come outside.

Trezini climbed out; while Delaney propped his shoulders solidly back against the wall, watching for any movement inside, his gun at the ready.

Through a quick mime, Delaney indicated that Trezini should climb over the wall and make his escape.

Both men were soaking wet already, and now Trezini was glaring at Delaney with water pouring down his scrunched-up face. After a moment, Trezini leaned in close to say, "You're coming with me!" He had to raise his voice to be heard over the rain, even at that short distance.

Delaney shook his head. "Go! Get as far away as you can, and call Agent Russell."

Trezini virtually yelled in reply: "The heroic thing isn't holding them off here alone, you moron! The heroic thing is being with me."

There was no time for arguments. Delaney cast his lover a mulish glance, but decided to let Trezini out-stubborn him. He nodded agreement.

But it was already too late – a man was creeping in through the bedroom door, gun pointing at the bed. While Delaney could make out enough to know he was there, it was too dark inside for the intruder to be a clear target. Not only that – Delaney and Trezini were at a disadvantage because it was somewhat lighter outside …

… and the man had seen them – he was swinging around, ready to fire.

Delaney shifted himself in front of Trezini to protect him – and at the same time Delaney fired three shots in a line across where he thought the man's chest should be. The window shattered.

The man got off a shot that hit the wall by Delaney's waist, but then he dropped to the bedroom floor, dead or dying.

"There's at least one more," Delaney shouted over his shoulder at Trezini. "Get over that damned wall!"

Trezini glared at him.

Delaney said, "I'll be right behind you. Go!"

At last, Trezini clambered up to the top of the wall and swung his legs over the other side. He was still balancing there on his stomach, though, when a second man entered the bedroom – Delaney fired a shot, and the man retreated, probably not for long.

Trezini called, "Come on, Josh! I'll cover you."

As Delaney scrambled up, the second man tried again, but Trezini fired at him until he fell. Hopefully, he'd been the last.

Delaney and Trezini dropped off the wall into an alley between the rows of houses. Lights shone in a few windows, presumably where neighbors had been woken by the gunshots, though no one had ventured outside, which was just as well; better to stay safely inside. Delaney was relieved to hear police sirens in the distance. He'd wanted a better response time to the alarm but he supposed there was no point in bothering over that yet.

The two men jogged along together, staying close to the darker side of the alley – remaining alert and careful, in case there were any more assassins. Just before they reached the cross-street, however, Trezini dragged Delaney out of the rain and into a shadowy sheltered recess, someone's makeshift shed.

Trezini stared directly at Delaney for a moment, almost nose-to-nose, searching for something – yearning for something. "We should just get the hell out of here," Trezini abruptly declared. "You and me on the run together. How romantic is that? I have money, Josh, enough to –"

Delaney was shaking his head, wondering where the hell this idea had come from, and suspecting he'd better put a stop to it while he could. "But they need you to testify at the trial."

The man was watching him, surprised. Disheartened. Mutinous.

"Angelo, please … that's what all this has been about. Hasn't it?"

A breath of time dragged by while Trezini considered his options. And then he sullenly surrendered. "All right. But we don't go in with anyone we don't trust."

"There's a squad car just down the road."

Trezini's hands clutched the cloth at Delaney's shoulders; apparently Trezini had trouble resisting the urge to shake him. "Don't you get it? Picano could have sent them to finish the job. It's always someone you know, someone familiar."

"But," Delaney stuttered out. "But – police officers?"

"How did those men get into the house, Josh?" Trezini asked, fierce and cynical all at once. "You tell me how they knew we were there, and how they got inside."

Troubling over this, Delaney felt the solidity of the very ground give way beneath him. Perhaps he had been naive once more. Wanting to know the honest answer, Delaney asked, "Do you trust Agent Russell?"

"Well, not that I have much choice – but, yes."

"Then we'll go find a phone, and we'll call him."

Trezini dropped his head in defeat and slowly sagged against Delaney, who gathered him up and held him while the rain pelted down around their little shelter. Delaney found that he didn't want to think too hard about what had just happened, or almost happened; and that in itself unsettled him.

After a long moment, Trezini reached into a pocket and produced a cell phone. He silently handed it over to Delaney, obviously still reluctant. And Delaney began punching in Agent Russell's home number.

Russell collected them personally, and took them back to the FBI offices. Valeri was waiting there, having been roused from her sleep by a phone call from the FBI agent. The four of them stood facing each other in a dim pool of light up one end of the dark open-plan office. Trezini and Delaney, wet through from the rain, were wrapped in blankets; Trezini was shivering, due to being cold or furious or both. All four were worried, which was currently being expressed by them angrily talking over each other. A few FBI people were loitering at the other end of the room, curious and tense and spoiling for action.

Valeri was insisting, "The point is, can we tie the shooters back to Picano? This could really help put him away; he's making it obvious he has something to hide."

"I bet they were from out of town," Russell said; "they might be difficult to trace –"

Trezini cut in: "Hey, Picano's not the only one involved here!"

Delaney offered a calmer explanation of Trezini's outburst. "It seems clear Matthew Picano has a source of information inside the Police Department. They knew where we were, and they knew how to get in without setting off the alarms."

Valeri looked from one to the other of them. "Well, who's the source, then? Do you have names?"

"Go put Genari on the rack," Trezini said, voice still belligerent. "He always dealt with the boys in blue. I don't know who was on our damned payroll."

Russell couldn't restrain his sarcasm. "There's something you *don't* know?"

And Trezini wasn't above biting back. "Don't take that fucking tone with me. Picano's the only one across everything and don't tell me you'd run it any different."

"Oh, there's some things I'd do very differently, believe me." Russell was staring very pointedly at Trezini; Delaney surmised that Russell wouldn't have welcomed Trezini into his own inner circle. Had the FBI agent been conditioned to view all homosexuals as security risks or people inclined towards betrayal?

Trezini was yelling at Russell now: "You were so hot to get Picano, you didn't even start looking at the mess in your own backyard. Why doesn't that surprise me?"

Delaney stirred himself. No one – least of all Trezini – could afford for the odd tensions between the four of them to fray. "That's enough," Delaney said firmly. "Both of you, that's enough."

Silence for a moment. One by one they each took a breath and began to calm down somewhat.

Quietly, Valeri asked, "All right, what next? What can we do tonight?"

"I'm taking them to another safe-house," Russell said; "a Bureau place. I've got people investigating the shooters." And he added in Trezini's direction, "People I trust." Delaney assumed that was both a challenge and an offer of peace.

Nodding agreement, Valeri said, "We'll meet there tomorrow. I've got an early date for the trial, we really need to push ahead on that. The sooner it's obvious that Picano is going down for this, the safer you'll be, Mr. Trezini."

Delaney was satisfied with the arrangements; however, he was surprised to find that Trezini was looking defeated again. Concerned, Delaney reached out to place a hand on Trezini's shoulder. But there was no time for questions or reassurances before Russell packed them off down to his car.

CHAPTER NINE

Russell drove Trezini and Delaney to a deserted factory and parked inside in the shadows. If this were mob business, Trezini dully reflected, he'd be damned worried right now. The three men got out of the car, and Russell led the way up a set of stairs to a row of offices and storage rooms that were solidly boarded up. It appeared that the safe-house was located inside. The factory loomed dark and empty behind them as Russell dealt with the locks and the security system.

While the exterior was distinctly unwelcoming, there had been some effort put into making the interior livable. It was undeniable, however, that the place was smaller and even gloomier than the previous safe-house. Russell secured the door, while Delaney watched. Trezini was beyond caring right now.

"The bedroom's through there," Russell said. "I'm going to stay the night, just in case. I'll be here on the sofa."

It looked to be a remarkably uninviting sofa. Trezini turned away to hide a serves-you-right-jerk smirk, though he muttered, "Never knew you cared."

Delaney was somewhat more polite. "Thank you, Agent Russell. We appreciate it."

And then Delaney's hand was laid firmly on Trezini's shoulder, repeating a supportive gesture he'd made back at the FBI offices, and Trezini was being ushered through into the bedroom.

The door closed behind them and Delaney went to turn on the solitary bedside lamp. The room was as cramped and unprepossessing as Trezini would have guessed it to be, but he couldn't find it in him to really give a damn. They'd had one hell of a night already. Not so long before, Trezini had been in complete possession of this most handsome of men, and it had seemed in that moment he had everything he'd ever dared to wish for. Such a perfect sense of satisfaction was doomed to be short-lived, though; that was no surprise. Trezini wasn't the naive one around here.

In silence, both men stripped off, and draped their damp clothes around the chair and across the floor, hoping they'd dry. Because they'd left the safe-house so precipitously, neither had anything to change into: they each got into the bed naked, and met in the middle.

Trezini was chilled all the way through, far too cold and too shaken to fall asleep yet, though he was exhausted. He figured Delaney must be feeling much the same way. They held each other bundled up face-to-face, even though it would be more efficient, for the sake of warmth, for one of them to curl around the other's back, spoon-fashion.

Delaney was gazing at him, into him, mute and concerned, confused and yearning. This seemed to be a time and a place in which confidences could be whispered. Trezini murmured, "I'm reconciled with God, I feel forgiven, but sometimes it's hard to hold on to the truth."

"You doubt what we're doing," Delaney said. It wasn't quite a query.

Trezini had, for one powerful moment that night, wished his life and his death were something other than what they were. But the moment had passed and he had chosen to follow the crusade once more. There could be no turning back, and it wouldn't be fair for Delaney to become plagued with uncertainties, so Trezini said, "No, I don't have doubts, Josh." He added, "I have fears."

"What scares you the most?"

"I don't fear dying. I want you to remember that. But …" Trezini let a shudder run through him. "But I fear that it won't be quick and clean. That he'll … cut off a thumb first. Or other parts of my anatomy. The heart and the cock that led me away from him."

"I won't let him get to you, Angelo, I promise." And Delaney was never more beautiful than when he was earnestly pledging himself, body and soul.

Trezini loved this man dearly. He hadn't expected this affair to be quite so genuine – and on both sides, too. "I'm scared you'll be hurt as well," he whispered. "I should never have dragged you into the middle of this."

A pained smile cracked Delaney's face. "That's my line, surely. I hardly knew what I was suggesting, when we first met in that freezer –"

"Redemption," Trezini said, as if it were the most fervent prayer, and would inevitably be answered. "Redemption."

Apparently lost for words, Delaney pressed a kiss to Trezini's mouth. They held each other tighter.

Trezini continued, "You don't mean much to him – it's my betrayal that Matthew feels, it's personal between us. But I don't want you to die, Josh, I don't want you hurt."

"Neither of us is going to die, Angelo." It seemed, however, that Delaney didn't have the heart to argue anymore. Grief coloring his face, he kissed Trezini again, an intense bruising kind of kiss. And then he quoted, "I will fear no evil; For Thou art with me."

"For Thou art with me," Trezini echoed.

"Sleep now," Delaney pleaded. "Sleep with me."

Trezini turned around within the warm comfort of Delaney's embrace. They curled up closer together than any two people could reasonably be, and they finally settled.

Russell left early the next morning, and returned a couple of hours later with Valeri and a suitcase packed haphazardly with Trezini and Delaney's belongings. This safe-house was even more uninviting in daylight than it had been in darkness. Trezini changed clothes, as his outfit was still damp from the previous night. He noticed that his dress-sense had become as casual and careless as Delaney's. Maybe he just couldn't be bothered anymore. No one was going to care, anyway: the four of them gathered together in the living area, all evidently having done without a restful night.

Eventually, once everyone had begun drinking their coffee, Valeri looked across at Trezini and said, "After last night, I'm sure you've thought some more about the Witness Protection Program."

That topic again. Trezini let out a sigh. "Forget it. There's no point even trying." But apparently Valeri was determined not to be shrugged off. "For a start," Trezini tiredly explained, "this is my neighborhood, and I don't want to live anywhere else. This place made me what I am."

"This place might destroy you, too," she reminded him.

"Yeah, maybe it will."

Delaney said, "I'd go with you."

Trezini found himself gaping a little, surprised by this offer of commitment, this *public* offer of commitment, and touched by it, too. Funnily enough, Valeri and even Russell seemed to be reacting a tad sentimentally this morning, no doubt due to the lack of sleep. "You would?" Trezini murmured, charmed by the idea despite himself.

"Yes."

"Thank you, Josh," he replied, in quietly heartfelt tones. But then Trezini spoke bluntly to them all: "No, I'm sorry, there's no point even discussing it. Picano's going to get to me sooner or later. So let's not go to the trouble."

Valeri said, "Maybe we want to go to the trouble, Mr. Trezini."

And it was good to know that he had won her loyalty but, right now, Trezini wasn't interested in dealing with anything other than reality. He suggested, "Let's just … concentrate on the trial, all right? And we'll see what happens. We'll see where we are at the end of it."

Eventually Valeri agreed with a reluctant nod. Russell appeared resigned to the worst. Delaney, though – he was staring at Trezini, and he looked profoundly concerned.

"Why won't you trust me?" Delaney demanded.

The man was as close to being in a temper as Trezini had ever seen him. Delaney's face was contorted with worry and frustration, and he was clattering angrily around the kitchen, preparing the two of them a makeshift meal. Trezini was leaning in the doorway, hands in his pockets, simply watching his lover.

Delaney cast him a glare and asked again: "Why don't you trust me?"

"I do trust you, Josh," Trezini replied in reasonable tones.

"I told you, I'll keep you safe. I promised you that."

"Yes, you did. And I know you'll try."

Delaney would not be reassured. Continuing to threaten the pots and crockery rather than Trezini, the man said, "Angelo. You have the strongest will of anyone I've ever met. *You* know that, *I* know that, *Picano* certainly knows it right now." Delaney twisted to fire directly over his shoulder at Trezini: "So, why don't you use that damned will of yours to make sure we do this without paying the price of your life?"

And people thought Delaney was naive, Trezini reflected ruefully. He murmured, "It's not going to happen that way."

A moment passed. Delaney dropped what he was doing, turned fully around, propped himself against the bench, and folded his arms across his chest as if he was cold. "We'll make a run for it," he pleaded at last. "We could walk out that door right this moment. You said you had money; we both have wits. We could stay one step ahead of them all."

"And live the rest of our lives as fugitives? Is that really what you want, Josh?"

"It could be …" the man began defensively. "Well, it could be romantic, like you said."

Tempting, very tempting. Perhaps Delaney would never know how close Trezini was to losing his resolve. But running away from the crusade wasn't going to work, and Trezini didn't even really *want* it to work that way. "No," he finally said. "That was a one-time-only offer. You should have taken me up on it then and there."

Delaney was so damned angry with him. "Yes," he spat out, "I should have." And he would have to live with the fact that he didn't.

They were obviously not going to reach an understanding about this. Delaney turned back to preparing the meal, though he was hardly in the mood to eat. Trezini sighed, and left him to it.

CHAPTER TEN

The first day of trying a case in court began the same way every time: along with a paranoid sense of never being quite prepared, Valeri always felt this buzz of excitement. Sometimes, as with this case, everyone around her was buzzing as well.

Journalists and members of the public were entering the courthouse with palpable anticipation. Everyone, including Valeri herself, was required to pass through a serious security check in the foyer, including metal detectors for the people and x-ray machines for their belongings.

Once Valeri and all her files were cleared by the guards, she wound her way through the various chattering groups and into the courtroom. The jury had been selected during three days of arduous arguments, compromises and minor victories. Today, counsel for the prosecution and for the defense would be making their opening statements; perhaps, when they were done, there would be time to begin hearing actual testimony.

The major players were assembling, and the public seating was quickly filling; and then everyone was rising as Judge Jovanovich entered his courtroom. The judge was an older man, with such a suitably grave and venerable appearance that he seemed to have been born for the role; he wasn't, however, an obviously sympathetic person. In the past Valeri had found him difficult to deal with, though ultimately fair.

The judge indicated that everyone should sit down, and then he called for the jury. Valeri watched them file into the courtroom, having gathered together in the secluded jury area in the warren of rooms on the next floor of the courthouse. As usual, there were twelve jurors and four alternates. Valeri was quite pleased with the selection: they were an attentive group of men and women, mostly in their thirties, and including a notable number of minorities. She didn't know whether to worry or not that the defense's strategy in relation to suitable jurors seemed to overlap the prosecution's strategy in a number of key characteristics.

The defense lawyer, Nathaniel Ripley, was an expensively-dressed middle-aged man, with an experienced and respectable presence. Picano had chosen well: not only did Ripley lend a sense of solidity to the defense, he was an excellent lawyer with many years of court battles behind him.

A worthy opponent, Valeri thought.

As for Matthew Picano himself, he appeared to be nothing more or less than a charismatic, reasonable and successful young businessman. He was, of course, sitting at the defense table next to his lawyer. The loyal and beautiful Nicola Picano was sitting in the front row of the public seating, directly behind her husband. They made quite a team.

While Valeri was proud to be prosecuting the case, she was also grateful that her boss, the Prosecuting Attorney, was sitting beside her, lending her his authority and support. In the public seating immediately behind the prosecution table were FBI Agent Russell, Lieutenant Eliot, and Delaney's former partner, Officer Watson. Russell and Eliot were abuzz with excitement, almost as much as Valeri was – but Robert Watson appeared puzzled and unhappy. Valeri hadn't met the man before today, so she had no idea what was bothering him. Wondering if the jury would pick up on it, or if they'd even find out who he was, Valeri was just about to draw Eliot aside for a quick consultation when the judge crisply banged his gavel.

Too soon – it always felt too soon – Valeri needed to clear her mind of such distractions, and concentrate instead on delivering her opening statement with sincerity and conviction. It was vital for her to show no fear: she must demonstrate that so-called ordinary people could safely stand up against the likes of Picano, at least within the justice system.

Valeri had decided to leap in to the heart of the case with both feet. "If Matthew Picano were nothing more than a legitimate businessman," she began in confident tones, "he would be a rich man with a number of successful and diverse businesses. But he's also a greedy man, who inherited a powerful organized crime network from his father. In one way or another he benefits from, or is responsible for, every crime that occurs in Chicago's West Side. We will show you evidence …"

Succinctly, she described the case she would be presenting, hoping that each element would remain clear in the jurors' minds, though very aware that the defense would do their best to dislodge and discredit it all.

"… Sometimes this evidence will seem complicated because Mr. Picano has hidden his ownership through a maze of companies and other people, but I am sure you will be able to see through the maze to the truth – and as a result I am sure you will find Mr. Picano guilty as charged. Thank you."

It was Nathaniel Ripley's turn. Valeri sat at the prosecution table, watching him, listening carefully, while maintaining a respectful expression tinged with mild skepticism. Ah, here was the groundwork of the defense's approach to Trezini.

"… and the main witness testifying against Mr. Picano is a man whose motives are, to say the least, rather suspect. Mr. Picano does indeed own a group of diverse businesses and he provides employment for a large group of very diverse people. But he is not responsible for everything that those people do. The prosecution's case is built on lies …"

Yeah, right, Valeri silently muttered. As if she'd have bothered to launch the trouble and danger and sheer *expense* of this case if it were all a lie. She had better things to do with her life. Nevertheless, the jury would be susceptible to seeing Picano as being persecuted rather than prosecuted, and Valeri would need to counter that with clear solid evidence, presented with a balance of reason and the nobler kinds of emotion.

Ripley's opening statement was as brief and pointed as Valeri's had been – in fact he timed it to run exactly five minutes shorter than her statement, no doubt deliberately. And then, too soon, Judge Jovanovich was saying, "Ms. Valeri, would you call your first witness?"

Valeri stood and announced, "The prosecution calls Carmine Trezini."

People were glancing towards the courtroom's main doors, but the court clerk brought Trezini in from the rear door that led to the judge's chambers. Delaney, looking smart in his police uniform, accompanied them. The court clerk escorted Trezini to the stand and handed him a Bible, while Delaney took up a discreet and protectively watchful post in the nearest corner.

Meanwhile Valeri was advising the court, "The prosecution anticipates that Mr. Trezini's initial testimony will be extensive. However, we reserve the right to recall Mr. Trezini to the stand throughout the presentation of our case."

The judge said, "So be it."

During the momentary lull in proceedings, Valeri couldn't help but glance surreptitiously at Picano. The man's expression was completely blank, though his attention was – not unexpectedly – fixed intently on Trezini.

The court clerk was reciting the usual formula: "Do you swear to tell the truth, the whole truth and nothing but the truth, so help you God?"

"Yes, I do," Trezini replied with no hesitation whatsoever.

Once he was seated, Trezini himself could no longer avoid glancing at

Picano. Valeri was pleased to see that Trezini's serious and confident demeanor didn't change. For that matter, Picano's blankness didn't falter, either; but Valeri knew something of the significance and the intimacy of this relationship. The two men stared at each other for a long moment, until Picano coolly turned away.

And then Valeri stepped forward to begin questioning her star witness.

Trezini was explaining things Valeri knew he had gone over a thousand times before, and yet his manner was professional and fresh. He maintained easy eye contact with Valeri and with the jury members, and he spoke in friendly tones. Though it was far too early in the trial to be certain of how this would affect the outcome, Valeri was pleased.

"So, on one hand I ran Carmine's," Trezini was saying, "which was a real nice bar, even if I do say so myself – and on the other hand, I ran the gambling den behind it. Mr. Picano owned both places; that's how he set things up, half legitimate and half illegal. He was smart, a real businessman. But, like Matthew often said, this is the nineties, this ain't Al Capone."

That last declaration was met with some amusement, which was good for their case. Picano remained scrupulously unmoved, though Valeri assumed that he wouldn't appreciate having his own jokes used in evidence against him.

The defense lawyer was, of course, on his feet. "Objection, Your Honor – that last comment is hearsay."

"Sustained," said the judge. It was too little too late, though: the jury had been amused, and would remember the matter.

Perhaps unaware that he really didn't need to, Trezini said, "Sorry, Your Honor," and his manner was genuine though easy, not overplaying it. The judge nodded gravely in acknowledgement.

While Valeri hid her untoward smugness from everyone except Trezini, she was *very* pleased with him.

The prosecution team was in the mood for celebration that evening. Through the court clerk, Valeri arranged for the use of one of the meeting rooms in the judge's chambers, and then she asked Russell to collect take-out Chinese. So, rather than send Trezini and Delaney back to their isolation in the safe-house, the two of them were now sharing a generous meal with

Valeri, Russell and Eliot. A security guard stood by the door, and the regular guards were on duty downstairs, but the courthouse was otherwise locked up and deserted. Everyone was in high spirits, though Delaney remained his usual quiet self.

Trezini, who was particularly exuberant, called out to the security guard, "Hey, buddy! You want to take a load off, and come join us?"

"Angelo," Delaney said, "the man has a job to do."

Ignoring Delaney, Trezini continued, "There's plenty here. Grab yourself a carton."

The guard looked around, and saw that no one but Delaney was making any objections. Valeri felt a little guilty for not backing up the cop, but she figured Trezini was as safe here as anywhere. After a moment, the guard walked over, selected a carton at random, snagged a pair of chopsticks, and then went back to his post, munching happily.

Trezini declared to the room at large, "I tell you, it's so damned good to be out of that house and *with* people."

Russell let out a happily cynical laugh. "Sounds like the honeymoon's over at last."

"Dream on, Russell," Trezini cheerfully replied. "Hey, it all went well today, didn't it?"

"Yes, it did," Valeri said. "I *knew* it was the right thing to do, going to trial."

Trezini and Delaney both seemed surprised by her comment. An uneasy pause lengthened. Delaney put down the carton of rice he'd just picked up, and asked, "Was there ever any question of it?"

Valeri cast about her, lost for words for the first time in a demanding day. Eventually she explained, "Well … I can't say I wasn't strongly encouraged along the way to make a deal, and agree to lesser charges."

Delaney looked mildly outraged – which for him expressed something close to the wrath of God.

"It's not as bad as it could have been!" Valeri protested. "At least no one influential was caught in Picano's dens during the raid."

Russell said in flat tones, "Oh, we made sure that wasn't going to happen."

"You *warned* people?" Delaney asked, horrified. "Where did that leave Mr. Trezini?"

"In your capable hands, Officer Delaney." Russell shrugged, as if it really wasn't an issue.

Trezini was just sitting there listening calmly to all this, barely even reacting. Even so, Delaney was seething with anger. Valeri supposed that to him it must appear as if the rest of them had put a high value on political expediency while disregarding Trezini's safety.

After long moments dragged by, Eliot made an effort to lighten the mood. "Joshua, this is certainly a long way from parking tickets." Her remark was met with some confusion, so Eliot continued, "Delaney used to be able to tell me exactly how many outstanding parking tickets there were in Chicago on any given day. It was quite an obsession, wasn't it, Joshua?"

Delaney was of course reluctant to be sidetracked; but he began to haltingly explain, and soon fell into what must have been his old spiel. "I never understood why people don't pay the fines. They know they're guilty, often they decided to take a risk and they lost. It's not that much money per ticket, but it all adds up. The police force is struggling with continual budget cuts, and everyone agrees that's a bad thing – but meanwhile there's all these outstanding fines. I had the idea that if we launched a public campaign, asking people to pay –"

Eliot was quietly laughing, apparently having heard this many times before. Russell was obviously asking himself, *We took this guy seriously?* Trezini looked about as perplexed as Valeri felt.

It wasn't that Delaney wasn't absolutely right – but surely there were larger and more meaningful issues to worry about. It occurred to Valeri to wonder what kind of frustrations were pent up beneath that equable exterior.

Delaney was looking around the table, seeing that no one empathized with his old obsession. Valeri was shocked to see tears on the man's face. Could Delaney really still care so much about the parking ticket situation, when he was now successfully working against Matthew Picano? "Joshua, my God," Valeri murmured – but Delaney was already talking again, trying to justify himself.

"Most people don't realize the size of it. There were well over one-hundred-fifty-thousand outstanding tickets last time I checked, a few months ago. That adds up to almost half a million dollars in uncollected fines. How many officers could the Police Department employ with those funds? The largest number of outstanding tickets for an individual was four-hundred-twenty-three. Why aren't we targeting … I mean, why is it that we can't …" And at last Delaney faltered to a halt.

No one else was saying a word, though they all obviously felt for him. Well, Russell probably felt for the poor guy, somewhere under the FBI Agent's macho embarrassment.

Delaney was openly weeping now, grieving.

"I know," Trezini said soothingly, getting up and going to the man, and wrapping him up in a hug. "I know." Delaney grabbed hold of his lover. Trezini whispered, "I know, Josh. Nothing will ever be the same again."

The two men held each other tight, apparently far beyond the shame of grasping after comfort, even though they were surrounded by gaping witnesses. Valeri was almost moved to tears herself.

Soon, however, Delaney made a visible effort to pull himself together and lighten up. Sensing the party was more than ready to break up, Valeri volunteered to drive the two men home. Russell, who normally performed such tasks when their regular driver wasn't available, had rarely looked more relieved.

The defense team had begun their cross-examination of Trezini. The former mobster was continuing to make a good impression this morning: he was stylishly yet subtly dressed, and appeared as comfortable as he'd been during Valeri's direct questioning.

No one seemed to pay any attention to Delaney, standing there near Trezini in his uniform, protective but unobtrusive. Perhaps provision of such a guard was assumed to be standard procedure in a case like this.

Eventually – inevitably – Ripley left a significant pause designed to regain any wandering attention, and then commented, "I am hardly surprised that the prosecution left it to me to raise the issue of your homosexuality, Mr. Trezini."

"I guess they don't think it matters," Trezini responded in easy tones.

However, everyone in court who already knew about this aspect of the case seemed to be holding their breath now; and those who didn't know were, to one extent or another, somewhat surprised. Valeri sat back and looked casually around, wanting to gauge reactions. She noticed that Officer Watson, Delaney's old partner, was no longer sitting in the vicinity of the prosecution table, and his face betrayed his distaste: Eliot had been intending to fill him in this morning, so he didn't hear it for the first time while in court.

The defense lawyer's manner was respectful, moderately accepting – and Valeri figured Ripley would be a fool to approach this any other way. "Is it something you'd rather hide?"

"I've never hidden it," Trezini said. "Well, not since I figured it out myself."

In exactly the same tones, Ripley commented, "Mr. Picano is an attractive man, is he not?"

"Ah, you noticed that, too?"

Amusement rippled through the court at this mildly teasing riposte.

The defense lawyer deigned to echo the amusement with a small smile and then let it die away before continuing. "It's an objective opinion that I've formed. I put it to you that your response to him is somewhat more subjective."

Trezini did not say anything in response.

"*Do* you find Mr. Picano attractive, Mr. Trezini?" Ripley asked.

A moment stretched. Valeri was glad Trezini felt able to take his time with this, though she found she was holding her breath.

Trezini turned slightly to look at Picano, who steadily returned his gaze; and then Trezini turned back to face the defense lawyer. "Yes," he said simply, as if he had no reason to deny it. And fair enough, too: Valeri herself thought that Picano was a handsome bastard.

"And yet Mr. Picano is a happily married man, he has a wife and children; he was uninterested in the way of life you offered him."

"I never made Matthew any offers."

Ripley's manner abruptly became harder. "I suggest that, resenting this man for not loving you, you turned against him and decided to destroy him."

"No," said Trezini. "That's not how it is."

"I suggest that your testimony against Mr. Picano was born solely of your own personal bitterness –"

Valeri was on her feet. "Objection, Your Honor –"

She didn't even need to state the grounds: the judge simply said, "Sustained. More questions and less remarks, Counsel."

"I'm sorry, Your Honor," Ripley said with a slight bow of his head. In reasonable tones, he asked, "Mr. Trezini, can you honestly tell the court you were never disappointed by Mr. Picano?"

Trezini took a moment to consider his words, and then he slowly offered a full explanation. "There was a time when, if Matthew had asked, I would have said yes. We were teenagers together, I was working out who I was – I don't figure that's so unexpected. He was always handsome. But he was never going to ask, I knew that. It's a long time since I felt anything for him but friendship."

"Friendship!" Ripley immediately protested. "You call this friendship – testifying against him with lies?"

Valeri surged to her feet. "Objection!"

Once more Judge Jovanovich simply said, "Sustained."

Given that she seemed to have his cooperation, and deciding that they'd already given the matter a reasonable airing, Valeri continued: "Your Honor, this entire line of questioning is irrelevant. The defense is trying to use an outdated homophobic attitude to turn our focus away from the actual crimes committed."

Still in protest mode, Ripley cried out, "*Homophobic?* I hardly think so. This man is openly gay – and Mr. Picano offered him friendship and employment for years, remained loyal to him since they were children together, welcomed Mr. Trezini into his home …"

"Objection," Valeri interjected. "That sounds like closing argument."

Judge Jovanovich said, "Be quiet, both of you."

Counting on his demonstrated outrage to see him through, the defense lawyer asked, "Why would the prosecution want to suppress this issue, if there's nothing to hide?"

"Enough!" Into the sudden silence, the judge asked, "Do you have any more questions, Counsel?"

"Yes, Your Honor," Ripley replied.

And the judge grudgingly indicated that he could proceed.

"Mr. Trezini, I believe you are currently in a relationship?"

Valeri had barely sat down before she was up again. "Objection! Relevance?"

Jovanovich considered this, but it seemed that he was curious. "Overruled, but get to the point, Counsel."

The defense lawyer nodded agreement, and turned to Trezini – who, without further prompting, simply said, "Yes, I'm in a relationship."

"With whom?"

Trezini hesitated a moment, as if used to some measure of discretion and privacy; but then he answered clearly, "Officer Joshua Delaney."

Ripley indicated the upright and unmoving Delaney: "The policeman standing there, watching over you?"

"Yes."

"And Officer Delaney has participated in building this ludicrous case against Mr. Picano?"

"Objection, Your Honor." This was ridiculous – Valeri wondered what Ripley thought he'd gain by such niggling tactics. Was he trying to provoke Trezini into a temper, perhaps? "Surely defense counsel is above characterizing the people's case as ludicrous."

"Sustained."

Trezini immediately began, "Yes, Officer Delaney is part of this. Testifying against Matthew Picano was something *I* decided to do, I'm trying to do some good for once in my life – but Joshua Delaney was the catalyst, he gave me the courage I needed –"

Ripley was of course trying to interrupt. "Objection! Non-responsive."

But Trezini was relentless. "– and I love that man. If I ever felt any lingering disappointment over Matthew, I sure forgot all about it when I met Joshua."

"Objection! Your Honor! I asked the witness no direct question."

"Overruled," the judge said once both men were silent again.

"But, Your Honor –"

"I'll allow Mr. Trezini's testimony to stand because you raised each matter he just addressed, Counsel." Jovanovich paused for a moment with his judicial brow raised, but Ripley didn't dare argue any further. "Now," the judge continued, "I believe a recess is in order for lunch. And when we reconvene, I suggest we move onto another topic."

The court clerk scrambled to her feet. "All rise." And everyone stood as the judge left through the rear door.

There was a collective sigh of relief once the judge had gone, as if that line of questioning had been problematic, in one way or another, for everyone in court. Trezini turned to consider his lover and Delaney immediately walked over to the witness box; Trezini began murmuring something with a wry grin, to which Delaney nodded in agreement, though his expression remained neutral.

Valeri discreetly considered the jury members as they began filing out of the courtroom. There were a couple of sympathetic or curious glances in Trezini and Delaney's direction, and a few quiet comments shared: it seemed the jury hadn't been too alienated either by Trezini's sexuality or by how the defense handled it. Perhaps Officer Watson was the person most offended: he looked bitter, as if figuring that he should have known all along that his former partner was a queer.

Everyone was milling around, thinking of nothing more serious than lunch. So no one really noticed when Nicola Picano walked calmly out of the public area and through the swing gates into the court-proper. Valeri caught sight of her out of the corner of an eye, though the attorney didn't make anything of the matter until it was too late.

Rather than going to her husband, Nicola walked right past the defense table and headed for Trezini – and there was a furious cast to her whole body. Valeri was up and moving around the prosecution table by now … Trezini lifted his head and saw Nicola approaching, but he didn't react as if she were dangerous.

Once she was close enough, Nicola lifted her hand and slapped Trezini hard across the face.

Delaney put himself bodily in her way before she could slap Trezini again; he made a point of not touching Nicola, but two guards belatedly ran over to restrain her. Nicola took the opportunity to spit on Delaney even as they began shifting her away.

Everyone had paused to watch this little melodrama unfold, reacting with bemusement or amusement. Picano was chuckling delightedly.

And then Delaney was hustling Trezini towards safety, out through the rear door. Russell caught up with Valeri, and they both followed after the two men.

Nicola was still obviously furious, squirming in the firm grip of the security guards; but on her way past, Valeri murmured to the guards, "It's all right – let her go." Once free, Nicola ran to Picano – Valeri turned to watch him take his wife into his arms, and hold her fondly, proudly. Well, the attorney thought; there was mileage to be gained here for both sides.

Trezini and Delaney were waiting in the corridors immediately behind the courtroom. Valeri and Russell joined them there, and the four of them stared at each other, startled by this unexpected attack on Trezini. And after a long taut moment, Trezini, Valeri and Russell burst out laughing at the pettiness of it.

Delaney, however, was deadly serious and very angry. "What the hell is so funny?" he demanded. "I let her get through. Angelo, I let her get through to you."

Trezini was barely able to talk over his laughter. "No harm done," he eventually managed.

"But what if she'd had a gun?" Delaney glared at his lover for a long moment. "Stop that and listen to me! I let her get close to you."

The other three began to calm down a little, for the sake of poor Delaney's sense of failure if nothing else. Trezini went over to Delaney and put a reassuring arm around his shoulders. "Never mind, Josh my love. You can get the next one, okay? You get the next one."

Delaney would not be so easily mollified, but Trezini led him off down the corridor. Valeri and Russell exchanged a wry glance, then followed.

Trezini was continuing, "Come on, let's see what's on the menu today. Nothing I'd have deigned to serve at Carmine's, I'm sure."

Of course, Trezini hadn't attended church since he'd gone into hiding; when he was in the mood for it, however, he participated in one of the televised services. He was doing so today, bowing his head in prayer along with the rest of the far-flung assembly, and then crossing himself.

Always respectful of such matters, Delaney was off to one side of the room, about as far away as he could get without withdrawing into their bedroom. The cop was performing his regular exercises with hand-weights, a thoughtful scowl on his face.

A hymn began on the television – delightfully enough, it was one of the hymns based on Psalm Twenty-Three. "Hey, Josh!" Trezini cried. "They're playing our psalm."

But the humor fell on oblivious ears. Delaney was looking at Trezini now, in a rather oddly focused way. After a moment, he said, "Angelo. Are you HIV positive?"

Where on earth had that come from? "No. Why?"

"The condoms. And …" Delaney searched around him for tactful words, but then grimaced instead.

"And my death-wish?" Trezini guessed. When Delaney nodded unhappily, Trezini continued, "No, I'm healthy. If it weren't for an abrupt case of lead poisoning in my immediate future, I'd probably live to a hale and cantankerous ninety-three."

Delaney said, "As a police officer, I'm required to have a complete physical every two years. I was cleared last time and there's only been you since."

"Well, it hardly matters if I go catching anything from you."

"Of course it matters," Delaney countered, his voice tight: "I intend to save you from the lead poisoning."

Trezini turned back to the television, though he wasn't even really aware whether the Mass was done or not; there were other things to trouble over. Eventually he said, "I wanted to protect you."

"From what? You just didn't want to ask me to trust you."

"Why should you take my word for it that I'm okay?" Trezini burst out. "And why should I have believed you? God, they're right – you *are* naive, Josh."

Delaney glared at him some more, sullen. It was patently clear that neither of them were satisfied with the conversation, but Delaney seemed as unwilling to continue as Trezini was. A difficult silence descended.

CHAPTER ELEVEN

Another day in court … The defense lawyer was cross-examining one of the bartenders who used to work at Carmine's. Valeri was sitting at the prosecution table, endeavoring to present herself as calm and composed. It wasn't so much the testimony causing her discomfort – the problem was that the air-conditioning was barely functioning. All around Valeri, people with flushed faces were fanning themselves and unbuttoning their collars, but she wanted to maintain a professional appearance if she possibly could.

By now, there were fewer journalists and almost no members of the public attending the trial. As the gallery slowly emptied day by day, the evidence table had conversely become more and more cluttered; it was currently piled high with bagged objects seized from the gambling dens.

"Then I'll ask you again," Ripley was saying, his tones impatient; apparently the stuffiness of the air was affecting his temper and delivery. "Did you at any time see Mr. Picano have anything to do with the gambling den?"

The bartender at last reluctantly answered, "I guess not. No." Nervous, the young man wouldn't even glance in Picano's direction.

"Did Mr. Picano visit the bar?"

"Yes," the man answered with a shade more eagerness. "And pretty much everyone who came to the bar knew about the den."

"That's not what I asked," Ripley complained.

Valeri hid a smile: it seemed Trezini had earned the loyalty of his staff. She was surprised at the idea that he'd been a good boss, though she supposed it shouldn't really have been such a shock. He was a pleasant person to spend time with, and often seemed to have a knack for smoothing rough waters – he even had a sense of fairness. It remained to be seen how the staff members' personal loyalty to Trezini weighed against their completely justifiable fear of Picano.

The bartender offered a further answer to Ripley's question. "Well, Mr. Picano would come to the bar in the evenings and have a drink with Mr. Trezini, quite often. I thought they were friends."

The defense lawyer took the opportunity to comment, "Having a drink with a friend who manages an establishment you own is hardly a crime, is it?"

Valeri got to her feet, though it was a real effort in these over-heated conditions. "Objection. Calls for a conclusion the witness doesn't have the expertise to make."

"Withdrawn," Ripley allowed, not even trying. He continued, "Mr. Trezini was responsible for running the bar that Mr. Picano owned?"

"Yes, I guess it was always Mr. Trezini who ran things there."

"So, as far as you're aware, Mr. Trezini ran both the bar and the gambling den?"

The bartender suddenly saw where this was going just as clearly as Valeri did. Reluctantly he told the truth: "Yes."

Ripley immediately followed this up. "And the income from the den – there must have been a lot of cash involved. What happened to that?"

"I don't know. Mr. Trezini handled the money."

"I see …" the defense lawyer mused, allowing the jury to draw their own conclusions. Well, he'd managed to make his point. Deciding to end on that note, Ripley announced, "I have nothing further for this witness."

Judge Jovanovich was as uncomfortable as any of them. Though it wasn't much past four in the afternoon, he limply lifted his gavel, let it fall and announced, "Recess. We'll reconvene at ten tomorrow." Everyone rose to their feet with a collective sigh of relief.

Delaney led the way out of the courthouse elevator and into the basement parking lot. Valeri had ensured that he and Trezini were brought here every day: ostensibly so that Trezini was readily available for advice or to give further testimony; though Delaney suspected Valeri was taking pity on them being confined to the rather unprepossessing safe-house. Instead of being cramped up together in a place with no natural light, they had the run of three connected rooms next to the judge's chambers, which at least had windows – though of course Delaney wouldn't let Trezini go near those windows even with the blinds partially drawn, for fear of sharpshooters.

As usual, their van was parked by the double doors leading to the air-conditioning plant. Delaney noticed that their driver was on his knees beside the vehicle, changing a flat tire.

Trailing along behind the cop, Trezini and Valeri were talking about the day's testimony. The attorney was explaining, "They're trying to cast doubts in the jurors' minds, they're trying to throw the blame back at you, Mr.

Trezini. It's nothing we weren't expecting."

"Sure, I guess it creates a reasonable doubt," Trezini replied. "Did the gambling den at Carmine's belong to me or to Matt? But with all the other dens as well, it must be pretty clear that Picano's behind them all."

"Yes, hopefully the strategy will end up as nothing more than a temporary distraction. Anyway, you know, if this fails, there are always the other charges pending. I can't see Picano and Genari getting away with murdering that man found in Lake Michigan."

Trezini murmured, "I wouldn't underestimate Matthew if I were you." Then he asked with somewhat more energy, "Hey, I've given you a sworn deposition about that, haven't I? You've got enough to proceed?"

Delaney silently and bitterly added Trezini's unspoken reason: … *in case anything happens to me.*

The three of them reached the van and the driver said, "Won't be long, Mr. Delaney. We got ourselves a puncture."

Restlessly loitering, Trezini tilted his chin at the double doors behind the van. "God, that air-conditioning system must be a hundred years old. What a racket!"

Valeri commented, "It was so stuffy in court today I thought I'd expire."

"It was the same back in chambers, though it always feels cramped there."

The plant was indeed rattling ominously away. Delaney looked around. The rest of the parking lot was deserted. He took a breath – and his cop-instincts shrieked the alarm. "There's a gas leak, too," he said. "Ms. Valeri, where's your car?"

Confused by his sudden urgency, she wordlessly indicated a sedan.

Delaney pushed Trezini in that direction. Over his shoulder, he called back to the driver, "Sam, get to security, tell them to shut down the plant, tell them there's a gas leak of some kind as well."

Valeri, Trezini and Delaney were already at Valeri's car. Sam was obediently running towards the security gate.

The gas level wasn't too high yet and the car was a relatively new one; Delaney told the others to shelter behind the next car along, and took the risk of leaning inside to turn over the ignition. There were no dire effects. So far so good. He said, "Ms. Valeri, you drive. But be prepared to do what I say."

Delaney grabbed Trezini and pushed him into the back seat, then got in after him. Valeri slid into the front: she only paused long enough to fasten her seatbelt before putting her foot down and taking the car out of the parking garage at speed. The gate was already open for them, no doubt at Sam's request.

For all his talk of doom and death-wishes, Trezini was compliantly following Delaney's orders. Right now Delaney wanted him out of view, so he hauled the man down to lie half-across Delaney's lap, and then leaned forward to shelter Trezini with his own body.

Though she was dealing with the situation, it was apparent that Valeri felt a little panicked: after all, she wasn't trained to handle this kind of emergency. Just as she was pulling out into the street, a truck bore down on them from out of nowhere – Valeri braked and swerved to avoid it, and then she just sat there, gripping the wheel too tightly.

"It's all right," Delaney said reassuringly. "We're fine, that was just bad luck. Now, Ms. Valeri, take a deep breath, and head for the FBI offices."

She nodded, and at last they eased into the traffic and drove away from the courthouse. Delaney looked around him as best as he could, trying to spot anyone taking an unwarranted interest in what was going on. But he couldn't see anything suspicious: those people who'd noticed their near-miss with the truck were already moving on. Delaney took a deep breath and decided they were probably safe for now.

"Thank you, Angelo," he murmured. And, sitting up straighter himself, Delaney added, "I think you can get up now."

But the man just wriggled around until he was comfortable, lying there on his back with his head and shoulders on Delaney's lap. "No, I like it down here," Trezini announced, looking up at his lover with a cheeky grin.

Delaney wondered if Valeri could tell through the rear-view mirror that he was blushing.

Standing close by, Delaney attempted to listen in while Agent Russell spoke on the phone to the security guards at the courthouse; however, the cop wasn't learning very much from Russell's monosyllabic replies.

Valeri was sitting in an office chair nearby, still looking a little shocked. A few FBI agents were scattered through the room, working. As for Trezini, he'd made himself comfortable again – he'd arranged two visitor's chairs over by a far window, and was sitting relaxed in one with his feet up on the other, gazing calmly up at a patch of sky.

At last Russell hung up the phone, and turned to face Delaney and Valeri. "They're just not sure," he announced. "Something in the air-conditioning plant was backed up, there were sparks flying. It could have been poor maintenance, and just a coincidence that the gas tank down there sprang a leak."

Delaney couldn't help but protest: "And our van had a flat tire, keeping us in the wrong place at the wrong time?"

"Okay, so your driver was in the habit of parking there. *But,*" Russell relentlessly continued, "it's almost too sophisticated to be deliberate. It depends on a lot of timing all coming together."

"Then you keep looking for anything that would have helped cause an explosion at the right time. Remember that court adjourned earlier than usual – though they might have planned for that, too. You should check the van to see if there was anything else done to delay us there."

A tense moment stretched. Perhaps Russell wasn't used to taking orders from a police officer. Eventually he commented with the lightest sarcasm, "You know, Picano lost his only guy with any finesse."

Delaney stared forbiddingly at the man. "This isn't a joke, Special Agent. Don't make the mistake of dismissing the danger: Picano's clever enough to set this up, and he can't afford to be obvious."

"He was being damned obvious, sending those shooters to the safe-house – and we still can't tie him to it."

"As Mr. Trezini keeps reminding us, it would be a mistake to underestimate that man."

"All right," Russell ground out, frustrated and angry in conflicting measures.

Tired, and deciding he'd made his point, Delaney gave up on Russell for now. He walked over to Trezini, and crouched close by him. "What are you doing?" Delaney murmured.

"Nothing," Trezini replied. "I'm just *being* ..." And he blessed his lover with a lazy smile. He seemed very peaceful, which was a pleasant change from recent days. The two of them managed to create a quiet moment together, ignoring the fact they were in company. Trezini continued, "Given that I won't be being for very much longer."

"Don't talk like that, Angelo."

Trezini's smile grew. "You're the eternal optimist, aren't you? You still hope we'll get away with this." Trezini reached a gentle hand to caress Delaney's face. "You're going to be hurt so bad when I'm gone."

Despite the shared intimacy, it took an effort for Delaney to confess, "I don't like to think about you dead and me alone, and all because I used you to get Picano."

"But this is my redemption, Josh; it's not you using me. Or at least it's both of us using each other. It doesn't really matter. We're doing a lot of good between us."

Delaney stumbled over the words: "I've spent my whole life trying to do the right thing, the best thing …"

"… and you've always been hurt for it?" Trezini guessed. "I'm sorry. You remember that, afterwards. Remember I was sorry it had to hurt you that much."

A silence passed. Trezini was so profoundly peaceful; Delaney wondered if this was what the man meant when he talked of feeling reconciled with his God.

Eventually, Trezini was the one to risk breaking the moment. "Can we go yet, Josh?" he quietly pleaded. "Why don't we go home, such as it is, and you can just be with me for a while? Let's just *be*."

Delaney nodded his solemn agreement.

There had been an afternoon back at the motel when Delaney had held Trezini this way. They'd been fully-dressed that time; though the clothes hadn't prevented them from directly meeting emotional need with simple comfort. This time they were lying on their bed and in each other's arms, both stripped naked.

Delaney had never before given himself over to such complete absorption in another person. Angelo gazed back at him, utterly defenseless; their mutual tenderness was a palpable thing.

Compared to such true communion, sex seemed virtually irrelevant. Nevertheless, at some stage in the darkest hours of the night they began making the gentlest of love together, perhaps seeking some way of grounding themselves in the physical world again.

"Are we going to get *any* sleep tonight?" Trezini murmured. It was close to dawn, and these were the first words spoken since they'd come to bed.

Delaney smiled. "We'll sleep all day in the judge's chambers instead."

"That's one of the things I like about you, Josh: you always have a plan." And Trezini surrendered without any further protest; though they did in fact fall asleep soon after.

Even Matthew Picano was weary of this trial; it felt never-ending.

Today featured a vital piece of testimony, however; something guaranteed to reinvigorate everyone's interest. Picano's main accountant, Jonathan Howe, was on the stand. And it was obvious that the man was feeling besieged by the prosecuting attorney's questions. Property deeds, company records, financial records and God-knew-what-else were scattered around, all being used in evidence against Picano. A whiteboard displayed the links of ownership between Picano and Carmine's bar, in terms so simple that even the jury could understand them. It was apparent that Carmine Trezini was nothing if not thorough.

Ironic, how Cat was demonstrating the very qualities that had been invaluable to Picano, at the exact same time Trezini was betraying his former friend. Picano had certainly had occasion recently to wish that his remaining inner circle were this thorough, this clever …

Such cool objective thoughts were useful to indulge while under the jurors' watchful eyes. Picano saved the fury and the hatred for less public moments, when his demeanor wasn't under such frustrating scrutiny. Imagine Matthew Picano's fate being in the hands of these twelve people who thought themselves his peers. Ridiculous. His father would have …

Well, Picano reflected, as Cat had often reminded him, this business wasn't Al Capone anymore. But, no matter what the jury thought, Matthew Picano wasn't anywhere near done yet.

Returning his attention to the proceedings with a sense of renewed reassurance, Picano found that Valeri had reached yet another conclusion. The woman's pace was slow and steady – and disturbingly relentless. "So," she was saying, "we've established that Mr. Picano owns Carmine's bar, and that he profits from the business managed there by Mr. Trezini, though the links are surprisingly indirect."

"Yes, ma'am," said Howe.

Valeri paused for a beat, and then continued on to her next step. "Tell me about the company called Sky Hook Holdings."

Howe reluctantly asked, "What do you want to know?" An admission in itself. Picano had known this guy would be worse than useless.

"What does it do? What kind of business does it conduct?"

"I'm really not sure," was the best Howe could manage.

Valeri lifted a brow; theatrical but not overly so. "You surprise me. Does it manufacture goods? Produce resources? Provide services? Invest funds?"

"I don't know."

She persisted. "But you are Mr. Picano's financial adviser, are you not?"

The weak-willed Howe stuttered out, "In … in most matters."

"Doesn't Mr. Picano own Sky Hook Holdings?"

"I don't know."

"What kind of business does Sky Hook Holdings conduct?"

Ripley was finally on his feet; Picano had been beginning to wonder what he paid this guy for. "Objection. The question was asked and answered."

"Your Honor," Valeri responded, "this witness is hostile to the prosecution."

The judge, who'd obviously been against Picano right from the start, simply said, "Objection overruled."

Picano didn't throw a poisonous look at his lawyer; he'd save that for later, when the look could be accompanied by some well-chosen threats.

The prosecutor was continuing, "Mr. Howe, I believe the company owns voting stock in a number of other companies. Is that correct?"

"Well, yes," Howe admitted.

"So, Sky Hook Holdings controls the business of other companies. Yes?"

"Yes."

Wonderful, thought Picano. Ripley had warned him they'd just have to ride this one out; Valeri had no doubt been saving Howe for her last witness so that she could finish on a damaging note. Despite the warning, though, this was almost worse to sit through calmly than Cat's testimony had been. Almost.

"Does the company have any other function?"

"I don't know," Howe muttered.

"Is Blue Skies one of the companies that it controls?"

"I don't know."

"Mr. Howe," Valeri said in a no-nonsense tone, "I have Blue Skies documents here with your signature on them. Need I remind you of the law relating to perjury?"

Howe scowled unhappily. "Well, I believe someone else owns the majority of Blue Skies' voting stock."

Huh, thought Picano, disgusted with the man. Anyone truly loyal to Picano would have chosen the perjury charge.

Valeri was on a roll now. "And that person in control of Blue Skies would be Mr. Picano's first cousin?"

Howe resorted to his stock answer. "I don't know." That was, of course, a lie – but he should have been better at lying than this.

"Does Mr. Picano own Sky Hook Holdings?"

"Perhaps he has an interest," Howe blurted out. "His stock portfolio is very diverse. That doesn't mean …" The man was floundering badly. He looked to Picano in desperation.

And that meant everyone else turned to look at Picano, too.

Well, who cared about guilt or innocence? Image was everything. Presenting himself as the most reasonable and sympathetic of men, Picano nodded encouragingly at Howe, indicating that he should just do the best he could.

Valeri turned on her heel and went on the attack again. "I understand that Blue Skies owns the property beside Carmine's bar. Is that correct, Mr. Howe?"

"I don't know," Howe said. And then he was blurting again: "Even if it does, that doesn't mean anyone profited from what went on there other than Trezini."

Oh yes. Picano would deal with this stupid man later.

"I have evidence here that suggests otherwise." Valeri was even smiling a little by now, though she was too wise to be smug.

Picano maintained his calm exterior, but it wasn't so easy when he felt prey to resignation for the first time. Perhaps the tide of this trial had just turned. Perhaps Valeri could sense victory.

But that didn't mean Matthew Picano was anywhere near done yet.

CHAPTER TWELVE

Delaney and Trezini were waiting through the day, as usual, in the chambers behind the courtroom. They were playing poker and, of course, Trezini was winning. Try as he might, Delaney rarely beat the man, which was no doubt due to what he thought of as Trezini's cunning. A hint of sunshine fell through one of the windows and across where Trezini sat; every now and then, especially while he was waiting on Delaney to make a decision, Trezini would tilt his face towards the light and close his eyes, letting it soak into him.

In just such a quiet moment, the door flew open and Valeri walked in, a jubilant expression on her face. "We've got him," she announced, "he's on the run."

Fearing he was gaping, Delaney asked, "Really? It's over?"

Valeri grimaced, conveying a quibble, though her grin remained strong. "Well, it's not *over*; this will drag on for a while, there'll be appeals. But he's on the way down and he knows it. Jonathan Howe's testimony just clinched it. If Picano weren't a fighter, his lawyer would be talking plea bargains with me right now."

Delaney didn't quite know what to do with this stupendously good news; he hadn't expected it yet, hadn't planned for it, even though it had been the desired outcome all along. Looking across at Trezini, Delaney was surprised to find that the ex-mobster appeared detached and uninterested.

"I was thinking," Valeri continued, "maybe you guys want to celebrate. You've been going stir-crazy in that safe-house. Why don't you take my car for the weekend, get out of the city? Doing it on the spur of the moment should be safe enough. I'll tell Russell."

"We'd appreciate that," Delaney replied. "Thank you, Ms. Valeri."

The woman tossed Delaney her car keys – as he caught them, she turned and left, still smiling broadly.

Delaney looked across at Trezini, puzzled by his lack of reaction. Surely everything had changed now, surely their crusade had been a success. "We did it, Angelo. Picano won't be able to stop the case."

Trezini finally met Delaney's gaze but when he smiled, it was a sad expression.

"He'd realize anything he tried now would be useless, so surely he won't bother. Other than legal appeals, as Ms. Valeri said." No reaction. Delaney continued, "As for revenge, that would be pointless and incriminating – and Picano isn't stupid. Right?"

"No," Trezini slowly said, "Matthew isn't stupid." At last the man stood, and began wandering towards the door, beckoning to Delaney. "Come on, then, Josh. Let's get the hell out of town."

And that suggestion was conveyed with something approaching a happy tone. Feeling reassured, and definitely excited to be getting away, Delaney smiled at his lover – and they headed out of the room together.

It was already late in the afternoon and Delaney felt reluctant to return to the safe-house. Once they were in the parking garage, he suggested, "Let's just go. We can buy what we need along the way."

Trezini agreed to this plan with a nod. He got into the passenger seat, but Delaney wouldn't even start the car until Trezini got his head down out of sight. "I'm no pretzel," the man complained.

"Then get in the back seat so you can lie down," he said, although this suggestion wasn't even dignified with a reply.

Delaney drove up out of the basement, through the security gate, and then pulled out into the traffic. Maintaining a casual air, he looked about him, but no one seemed to be paying them any attention. He didn't see anyone he recognized as linked to Picano. Robert Watson was loitering on the front steps of the courthouse but apparently he didn't notice his old partner driving by.

As the car reached the end of the block, Trezini sat up straight again. Even though Delaney would have preferred him to stay hidden for a while longer, the cop didn't bother protesting or complaining. There was so much traffic around them, surely one car would be lost in the midst of it … Delaney worked his way across into the fast lane, and headed for the freeway.

They'd reached a T-intersection in the middle of nowhere, with no signs or anything else to indicate which way they should go. Trezini suspected Delaney had been driving in random directions anyway, so it really didn't matter; the weather was fine, and the countryside was peaceable. He sat there in the passenger seat, relaxed. Happy. Trezini sent a silent prayer up to God, thanking Him for this unexpected happiness.

Delaney was sitting there, leaning forward over the steering wheel, looking up and then down the road, obviously lost. Breaking the comfortable silence, he at last asked, "Which way, Angelo?"

"I don't know," Trezini replied.

"Well, what's out here? Where's the nearest town of a decent size?"

"I don't know that, either." When Delaney lifted a skeptical brow, Trezini continued, "I've rarely been outside the city; and when I have, I usually left via O'Hare."

After a moment Delaney nodded his understanding. "We'll go right," he suggested.

"Left," Trezini countered, for the sake of argument.

And Delaney put the car into gear, and turned left. It didn't really matter, after all, and there were few signs of civilization out here to guide them. They drove on, surrounded by a flat landscape and bucolic green, under a high arch of blue sky. Time passed, and the sun slowly lowered towards the far horizon.

"Are you speeding?" Trezini asked.

"No. I haven't been, because we don't want anyone taking any notice of us."

"Good, because there was a cop car back there."

"I saw it."

The police car had been tucked away behind some bushes, presumably conducting a speed-check. Though Trezini wondered how much attention the cops were paying to the minimal traffic: one of the officers had been chatting into his radio handset, feet up on the dash. Trezini observed, "Well, they must belong somewhere. I guess we're not in the middle of nowhere, after all."

"Yeah," Delaney agreed.

And, sure enough, they soon found themselves driving into a town. To his own surprise, Trezini said, "I'm starving, Josh. Let's get something to eat; something good, if we can."

Delaney glanced at him, aware that Trezini hadn't had much of an appetite for weeks now. "Sure," Delaney murmured, a tiny smile on his lips. "Sure."

It might have been luck that led them to this place; Trezini preferred to think instead that his lover was skilled at making the best of things happen. Delaney had found them a restaurant, and not just any old restaurant – this one was more than pleasant, and the food had been worthy of Carmine's.

The evening remained warm, so Trezini and Delaney had eaten outside in the restaurant's courtyard, surrounded by breeze-rustled trees and capped by a magnificent night sky. Trezini leaned back in his chair and sent another contented little prayer up to God. He didn't even care that their table was still strewn with the detritus of their meal; such service could be excused when the waiter was distracted by a murmured conversation with another group of quietly happy customers.

Even the usually stoic-faced Delaney seemed to almost be glowing. Eventually – once he'd finished his second coffee and set the cup down, and contemplated the world around him with evident satisfaction – Delaney leaned forward, and whispered, "Angelo … perhaps we should go find a hotel."

Trezini couldn't help but chuckle. "Oh yeah," he replied. "I'm flattered, Josh. We've been let out for the first time in months, and all you want to do is rush me back inside again."

Apparently despite himself, Delaney's mouth was curling into another tiny smile. "I was just thinking it's getting late," he dissembled, "the front desk will close, we won't be able to check in."

Casting the man a skeptical glance, Trezini was completely disarmed when Delaney's smile grew into an honest and lascivious grin. Trezini couldn't help but smile in response: Joshua Delaney had never looked at his lover in quite that way before. The two of them still had so much to explore of each other …

Trezini sat up and waved a peremptory hand to draw the waiter's attention. "Josh, it's getting late," he declared, "and I think we should go find ourselves a hotel room while the front desk is still open."

Valeri and Russell each seemed to have something that needed saying, so without too much overt maneuvering they agreed to go to the bar together to buy a round of drinks, leaving Valeri's partner Jeffrey and Russell's date Ursula to keep each other amused. As soon as they were out of their companions' earshot, Valeri said, "You don't think Trezini and Delaney should have gone."

Russell shrugged. "We're celebrating," he said. "Forget the gloom and doom."

"Doom?" Valeri stared at the man, knowing he wasn't one to exaggerate. "Is it really so dangerous for them?"

Instead of answering, Russell gave their order to the bartender.

Valeri persisted: "A spontaneous decision to just go like that, no one even knowing they're out of town except you and me. In effect, they've disappeared. Picano's people would have to be watching pretty closely to even notice."

"We shouldn't underestimate him, remember?"

"My God," she muttered, beginning to suspect she'd done the wrong thing.

Russell was watching her closely. "Well, don't go assuming the worst just yet. Trezini agreed to it, right?"

"Yes."

"He knows these people; and he sure as hell has a feel for what's safe and what isn't."

"Oh, of course," Valeri agreed, immediately feeling a bit better. "We can trust him to know what's best."

Carmine Angelo Trezini was a tenacious man; resolute in seeking whatever he wanted, whether that was his crusade against Picano or his love for Joshua Delaney or his continuing survival. Except, Valeri reflected, Trezini seemed so certain he wouldn't be needing the Witness Protection Program. Unless that was simply something he couldn't be bothered thinking about until he really had to, given that he'd be leaving his home and his community behind. Really, Valeri could interpret the situation a number of ways; Trezini was a difficult man to figure out.

When Valeri looked up at her companion, she caught an unguarded frown on Russell's face that matched her own. "Since when did you start caring?" Valeri asked.

Russell just grimaced at her.

Trezini and Delaney were making love.

They had so much yet to explore of each other *physically*, let alone in matters of likes and dislikes, personality and spirituality. There were so many things they hadn't done. The few months of their affair had flown by, and the two of them hadn't really developed much range, with a notable exception or two. Tonight, for example, an occasion on which Trezini would have assumed he'd want something complicated and sophisticated and memorable – tonight he and Delaney were jerking each other off.

But, with Joshua, the simple could be astoundingly profound. And the simple could be wonderfully fun, too. How could Trezini ever ask for more than that?

They were lying there on their hotel bed, thoroughly naked, having discarded everything but the lower sheet, and having left the curtains wide open so that the night sky and the moonlight became their witnesses. Delaney was lying there beside Trezini, propped up on an elbow and smiling down at him; Delaney's hand was gentle and firm on Trezini at once, both bestowing and prolonging pleasure. How had this innocent man learned so quickly?

Trezini recalled the confusion, the ignorance with which Delaney had received Trezini's first kisses. And then the man's good-natured blundering attempts to return those kisses when he'd feared Trezini would freeze to death, standing there propped against Delaney, wrapped up in the man's arms … It seemed a lifetime ago. So much had changed since then.

Delaney was leaning down now to kiss Trezini with all the skill and care he'd devoted to taking care of anything and everything Trezini needed. There was genuine love in Delaney's expression. And that in itself was plenty memorable enough. Trezini surrendered himself thoroughly, wondering vaguely at the strange notion that he was truly giving Josh everything for the very first time.

It was Saturday; nevertheless, Valeri was woken early by the phone ringing. Beside her, Jeffrey buried his head under the pillow, wanting only to remain asleep. Wanting only to join him, Valeri nevertheless picked up the receiver. "Yes?"

"It's Russell," came the heavy, unwelcome voice. "Bad news. Jonathan Howe died in a car wreck last night."

Valeri abruptly sat up in the bed, curling her legs under her. "My God … Was it an accident?"

"Looks that way, but we've got to assume otherwise."

"Trezini …" Valeri murmured, fear and guilt clutching at her heart.

"I tried calling, but his damned cell phone's turned off." Russell sounded angry, and as worried as she was. "Did they say where they were heading?"

"No, and I didn't ask. It seemed safest to just let them go."

"I'll put out an APB. You get in here out of harm's way."

Valeri didn't have time to respond before Russell hung up. The dial tone sounded harsh in her ear. She settled the receiver back on the phone, then shifted to the side of the bed and fumbled for her robe while her feet tried to locate her slippers.

Then she turned around to shake Jeffrey's shoulder – he was still lying there, but his eyes were open, watching her, no doubt hearing how troubled she felt. Valeri tried to offer him a smile. She wanted him out of harm's way, too, so she said apologetically, "Time to get moving, honey."

Delaney was discovering what it meant to be utterly content. There was plenty to concern himself about, of course, but he and Trezini had managed to leave such worries behind in Chicago. For now, the sunshine was warm, the blue sky was infinite, the breeze was soothing, and nothing else could possibly matter.

Ms. Valeri's car had been running low on fuel, so they'd found a gas station stranded in the middle of all this level countryside. Once Delaney had filled the car up, he began washing the windshield. Trezini waited there quietly, leaning against the rear of the car, looking about him. The two of them could have been entirely alone in the world; Delaney found the odd thought rather pleasant.

Obviously not wanting for space, the pumps had been placed a fair distance from the gas station's general shop and service booth. The only indication that Delaney and Trezini did have company was a hint of movement inside the booth; presumably the attendant. The gas station had been placed at an intersection. There were a couple of houses and barns located in the other three corners formed by the meeting roads but otherwise, only fields and undeveloped countryside stretched around them.

Delaney finished up and began heading towards the shop. Already a few steps away, he paused and called back to Trezini: "Do you want anything? I'm getting a drink."

Trezini, who'd seemed lost in thought for much of the morning, seemed a little distracted now, a little uneasy. "No," he eventually replied, with a sketchy smile. "No, I'm fine."

Yes, Angelo, you are fine, Delaney silently agreed, returning his lover's smile in full measure. And then he turned away and walked towards the shop.

There had been a car engine idling somewhere on the periphery of Trezini's hearing; it was so faint, though, that Delaney hadn't noticed it, or at least the man hadn't attached any significance to the sound. So be it, Trezini thought; everything would be better this way.

Trezini watched Delaney's stride for a moment; enjoying his lover's confidence, his certainty, his strength. The other car was no longer idling, no longer waiting.

Looking vaguely about himself, Trezini slowly walked a short distance away from the gas station. The sunlight blessed him but he folded his arms across his chest, feeling cold all the way through. The car was drawing closer. And Delaney had entered the shop now, and the door had swung closed behind him with a muffled thud.

Trezini was alone. He took another step away, and then another.

Delaney stood before the triple doors of the refrigerator, trying to decide between twenty brands of bottled water and a hundred varieties of fruit juice. The attendant, who hadn't responded to Delaney's greeting, was loitering at the far end of the shop, not even bothering to wait for his customer at the till.

Considering what he could buy that Trezini would most like, Delaney glanced back through the windows. Trezini had wandered off, face turned up towards the sunlight; his forever mutable expression, at this distance, seemed quite blank. Delaney returned his attention to pondering the contents of the fridge.

It occurred to Delaney that he could hear a car approaching. There had been so little traffic in the area that this in itself was noteworthy. Delaney glanced outside again, looking for Trezini, who'd wandered further away …

… and Delaney abruptly sensed that something was about to go horribly wrong.

He'd known what was coming. Angelo had always known. He couldn't shake the coldness, though, and he couldn't quite deny an icicle of fear, a hollow of regret.

But, at last letting his arms fall to each side, Trezini found himself able to stand tall and easy. He prayed: *Our Father, who art in heaven, hallowed be Thy name …*

The car was by now an ugly roar.

Delaney dropped whatever it was in his hands, heedless of anything but Trezini. Glass shattered behind him as he ran for the door.

A car was driving past, a gun aimed out through an open window. Too late, he'd be too late, despite his legs pushing him forward at a speed he'd never reached before. Two men in the car, and Trezini just standing there, Trezini just waiting there. He'd said all along it would come to this. *No!* But Delaney didn't waste breath protesting – he just ran.

Too late.

The gun fired once, twice, thrice.

And Trezini fell back in the dirt, arms wide, as graceful in this as in everything he did.

At last Delaney reached him. Blood and bullet-holes were an obscenity across Trezini's shirt. The only sounds in the world were the car fading away, and Trezini panting for air. Delaney fell to his knees beside his lover. Silence now, but for those short gasping breaths.

Too damned late. Delaney widened his legs to encompass Trezini, and lifted the man's head and shoulders up to rest against his thigh.

Trezini lay there in the sunlight, fighting for breath; Delaney was already feeling torn apart by an impossible yearning desperation. This couldn't be happening, this *shouldn't* be happening … The two of them stared at each other, sharing these last moments.

Not wanting to burden their parting with his own bitterness and guilt, Delaney began reciting their psalm – speaking silently, though he could swear Trezini was reciting it, too – *Yea, though I walk through the valley of the shadow of death, I will fear no evil; For Thou art with me.*

Delaney lifted a hand to lovingly caress Trezini's face. This man had become Delaney's whole life and Delaney was glad that it had been so. Another caress of that bold-featured face, that close-cropped hair; and with this last blessing, Trezini finally quit fighting. He took one easy breath, and then a shudder ran through him. Delaney gathered his lover up into his arms, feeling a ragged groan of incomprehensible loss force its way out of him and echo into emptiness. The shudders ceased … and Carmine Angelo Trezini was gone.

A brief time passed. Delaney clutched Trezini close, pressing his face against the man, throat aching, silent again. He was vaguely aware that the gas station attendant had ventured out of the shop, and there was someone who'd come out of a house across the road, but they kept their distance, not intruding.

Eventually, too soon and too late, Delaney let his lover go. He gently lowered Trezini to lie alone in the dirt and the beneficent sunlight; he dragged fingertips over those beautiful green-hazel eyes to close them for the last time; and then Delaney stood up. The grief was awful, but he bore it, damp-eyed and numb-hearted.

And Delaney walked away. There wasn't anyone like Trezini, there never had been and never would be: the world was bleaker for this untimely loss. Delaney walked, not caring where, not even bothering to follow the road. He felt as strong and as determined as he ever had, but he was so terribly alone now. Joshua Delaney could do anything he wanted, anything at all.

Except put things back the way they were.

ABOUT JULIE BOZZA

Ordinary people are extraordinary. We can all aspire to decency, generosity, respect, honesty – and the power of love (all kinds of love!) can help us grow into our best selves.

I write stories about 'ordinary' people finding their answers in themselves and each other. I write about friends and lovers, and the families we create for ourselves. I explore the depth and the meaning, the fun and the possibilities, in 'everyday' experiences and relationships. I believe that embodying these things is how we can live our lives more fully.

Creative works help us each find our own clarity and our own joy. Readers bring their hearts and souls to reading, just as authors bring their hearts and souls to writing – and together we make a whole.

I read books, lots of books, and watch films. I admire art, and love theatre and music. I try to be an awesome partner, sister, daughter, friend. I live an engaged and examined life. And I strive to write as honestly as I can.

I have lived in two countries – England and Australia – which has helped widen my perspective, and I have travelled as well. I love learning, and have completed courses in all kinds of things. My careers have been in Human Resources, and in eLearning and training, so there has always been a focus on my fellow human beings and on understanding, conveying, sharing information.

Knitting gives me some down time and the chance to craft something with my hands. Coffee gives me stimulation and a certain street cred. My favourite colour has segued from pure blue to dark purple, and seems to be segueing again to marine blues.

I think John Keats is the best person who has ever lived.

And that's me! Julie Bozza. Quirky. Queer. Sincere.

If you want to know more, please do come find me at juliebozza.com and libra-tiger.com.

OTHER TITLES BY JULIE BOZZA

The Butterfly Hunter Trilogy:
    Butterfly Hunter
    Of Dreams and Ceremonies
    Like Leaves to a Tree
    The Thousand Smiles of Nicholas Goring

Albert J. Sterne:
    The Definitive Albert J. Sterne
    Albert J. Sterne: Future Bright, Past Imperfect

The Apothecary's Garden
The Fine Point of His Soul
Homosapien … a fantasy about pro wrestling
Mitch Rebecki Gets a Life
A Night with the Knight of the Burning Pestle
A Threefold Cord
The 'True Love' Solution

Anthologies:
    Call to Arms
    A Certain Persuasion
    A Pride of Poppies

www.ingramcontent.com/pod-product-compliance
Lightning Source LLC
Chambersburg PA
CBHW070500170726
48291CB00008B/2590